Hot Scots, Castles, and Kilts

Hot Scots, Castles, and Kilts

Tammy Swoish

DELACORTE PRESS

Published by Delacorte Press
an imprint of Random House Children's Books
a division of Random House, Inc.
New York

Visit us on the Web! www.randomhouse.com/teens

Educators and librarians, for a variety of teaching tools,
visit us at www.randomhouse.com/teachers

Library of Congress Cataloging-in-Publication Data
Swoish, Tammy.
Hot Scots, castles, and kilts / Tammy Swoish. —1st ed.
p. cm.
Summary: Sixteen-year-old Sami and her romance-writer mother
spend a month in Scotland fixing up an old farm as a tourist
destination, while Sami and her new friend Fiona hunt for the resident
ghost and Sami helps resolve a centuries-old feud.
ISBN 978-0-385-73447-9 (trade) —ISBN 978-0-385-90450-6 (glb)
[1. Clans—Fiction. 2. Families—Fiction. 3. Ghosts—Fiction. 4. Farm
life—Scotland—Fiction. 5. Scotland—Fiction.] I. Title.
PZ7.S98254Ho 2008
[Fic]—dc22
2007024312

The text of this book is set in 12-point Cochin.

Printed in the United States of America

10 9 8 7 6 5 4 3 2 1

First Edition

This book is dedicated to my Sammantha, without whom I wouldn't have had a character to send to Scotland.

Day 1

Summer Vacation

Barf Bags

What creative genius coined the phrase barf bag? They should've gone with something more sophisticated, like vomit vessel or regurgitation receptacle.

Takeoff, plus turbulence, plus air sickness equals me and my new close friend, the barf bag. I took Mom's bag too, just in case.

Flying sucks.

Mom and I have been on this plane for five gross hours. I've been nauseous, couldn't eat, barely watched a movie, and tried to sleep. No luck.

Molly MacKensie, a long-lost Scottish relative of Mom's, has invited us to spend a month and a half with her this summer. We're going to visit our ancestral homeland, Scotland.

Who knew we were Scottish? We're German, French, and Polish. But Scottish? No one tells me anything. My parents keep secrets from me like they're high-ranking officials in the CIA.

I've seen television shows about the Loch Ness monster. What's the deal with that? An ancient sea creature living in a freshwater lake? Sweet!

Maybe I'll see it. Maybe I'll be standing onshore, snapping pictures, and the huge beast will appear, showing itself to me. Then it will lean in real close, breathe fire at my feet, and roar like a crazed medieval dragon, swinging its gaping, razor-tooth-filled mouth at me. I will freeze in terror, hoping to not pee my pants.

But a gorgeous knight, wearing a kilt, will come to my rescue. He'll hold his broadsword high and say, "Auch, Nessie, leave the bonnie lass be." The monster will obey his command and slither back into the dark waters of the lake, leaving me, knees shaking, in love with my hero.

I sighed, gaining control of myself. Mom says I'm overly dramatic. Dad calls it passionate. I like to think of it as creative.

I've spent the last month of my sophomore year of high school researching and preparing for this trip.

Everyone is so hyped about it that Mom and Dad even threw a Scottish-themed sixteenth birthday party for me.

Try explaining to your friends the fat man standing in the corner of your yard wearing a kilt and playing a bagpipe—which, by the way, sounded like a dying cat. It was all I could do to keep myself focused long enough to blow out my candles.

So now Mom and I are off to spend forty days in Scotland.

Relatives, castles, superstitions, ghosts, and, hopefully, hot guys.

Molly, Mom's newly discovered relative, has a fifteen-year-old daughter, Fiona. I wonder what they're like. Mom assures me they are not weirdos or anything, but she has an odd, writer's personality, so I'm not too cool with her as a judge of character, although she is always telling me her written characters are very realistic. I guess what she's trying to say is that she has to know and understand people to write them.

I read one of her romances once. Mom's about as in touch with reality as someone who claims to have fallen in love at first sight.

I guess Fiona and I should get along since we're both in our mid-teens. And I have a lot to say on the topics of guys, makeup, and shopping. Trust me.

3

Before leaving home, I went to the mall and strategically purchased clothing for the Highland weather. I bought hiking boots, jeans, sweaters. . . . I did not buy anything plaid. First, it doesn't suit my light complexion and dark hair; and second, what if I mistakenly bought a rival clan's plaid? I've read about clan feuds, and I don't want to be on the receiving end of some medieval revenge feudy thingy.

10 p.m.

A summer romance would be awesome. I'm single. I broke up with Chad last week 'cause his hands are girly.

And long-distance relationships are a pain.

Not that I've ever had one.

10:10 p.m.

It'd be so cool to go back home and tell all my friends that I'd dated a hot Scot. If it happens, I'm taking a ton of pictures and plastering them all over my Web page. Then if no one asks me to the winter formal, I'll say something like "We decided not to date other people."

10:23 p.m.

The BF-in-another-country angle could make me a hot commodity with the guys at home. Untouchable — and the untouchables are, ironically, always the girls the cool guys want to date. Then maybe they'd walk around with that fine, forlorn love pout because of *me* for a change. Sweet.

11:01 p.m.

Mom has talked enough about her romance novels set in Scotland for me to know that Scottish men have steamy bodies and come-hither charm, whatever that means. But, since they do, I splurged on beauty products.

Mom's always saying, "Sami, you spend too much money." But, hey, I'm a teenage girl.

I'll find a job when I get home. Then Mom won't moan about how I spend money because it'll be *my* money.

12:15 a.m.

The Internet said that the weather in the Highlands in July would range from sixty to seventy degrees during the day, but that it would be a lot cooler at night.

I hope the MacKensies have heat. From the pictures I've seen, most of the buildings there are pretty medieval-looking, made of stone and all. Medieval buildings are cold and damp and heated with fire-places. I read somewhere that they used to burn animal poop. Gross. That smell would never wash out of my hair.

1:05 a.m.

How long is this flight?
    Will I have jet lag?
    Maybe not if I sleep.
    I'm going to sleep.

1:57 a.m.

Can't sleep.
    Anyone for a game of cards or something?

3:03 a.m.

Mom is snoring. I want to die. This is so embarrassing.

I hope the Brad Pitt twin two rows back doesn't think it's me.

What if Mom drools?

Gross.

4:27 a.m.

Trying to sleep is futile.

I dug through Mom's bag and pulled out her Scotland travel guide. I didn't care about the maps, motels, or restaurants. I turned to the second half of the monster-sized book, the interesting stuff.

Along with dinosaur-like creatures living in the lakes, spirits and goblins apparently run rampant in the countryside. The section on haunted castles has to be at least thirty pages, each full of detailed sightings.

I wonder if MacKensie Castle is haunted? That'd be sweet.

Cool! There is apparently a long tradition among Scottish people of foretelling the future. Maybe I'll get in touch with my Scottish self and hone my Second Sight skills.

Customs—YES!

My first trip through customs: a life experience marker. Here I was stepping onto foreign soil (well, technically I was already on foreign soil, but still) and I didn't even get a stamp in my passport, just a slip of paper.

How do you say "let down" in Scottish?

It was nothing like in the movies. No huge guy dressed in a dark suit whisking us into a small room to rifle through our belongings, question us under a single, hot lightbulb, or threaten to throw us in prison.

Scottish people are too mellow with their country's security, but they do sound cool . . . if they'd just slow down enough for me to actually understand.

Family Reunion

Molly and Fiona met us at Inverness Airport.

You know that weird stuff about everyone having a twin somewhere in the world?

I think Molly is Mom's twin.

I swear.

They both have the same reddish-brown curly hair. Once, I tried to copy the shade and curl of Mom's hair, and let's just say that ended badly. I figure I should save myself countless futile attempts and potential disasters and just resign myself to the fact that I'm stuck with straight, fine, dark brown hair.

Mom and Molly have the same perfectly shaped hazel eyes. Top those off with identical smatterings of freckles across their small noses, and people at the airport were stopping to stare at the "twins."

They hugged, laughed, and talked. Then they even started to finish each other's sentences. Weird.

What if Mom's long-lost relative is some psycho fan or something? After all, Molly contacted Mom through her author Web site. Mom publishes using her maiden name, Patty MacKensie, but our real last name is Ames.

Molly hugged me. I didn't get any funky feelings, so I guess she's not the stalker type.

At least I hope.

Fiona is WEIRD

Mom and Molly are the only creepy, family-like connection.

I'm light, but Fiona is almost albino.

I wear makeup, and Fiona doesn't.

I wear jeans, and Fiona wears denim that looks like it was purchased at a dollar store.

How can I communicate with someone who obviously doesn't shop at American Eagle?

My nails are painted; Fiona's are plain and clipped.

I'm tall, and Fiona is short.

I smiled . . . and she smiled . . . and then we said hello at the same time.

Maybe I'm just tired and cranky.

Castle in the Mist— Whatever

More like a cloud of freezing, heavy air than mist— but it's not a castle.

Hey, where's my castle?

It's a croft, with a stone cottage strategically placed in the middle of a stinking field. There's a low stone wall surrounding the structure, but sheep are walking through an opening in the wall and grazing right in front of the door.

Molly said this is where Mom and I will stay for the next month.

Ummm...Hello

There's no electricity.

We have to pump water into the sink in the kitchen.

Are we in the Stone Age?

Geez. Even the Romans had running water in their homes. Of course, during the height of the Roman Empire, this part of the world was run by uncivilized, dirty barbarians.

Molly and Fiona left us to settle in. Molly offered to pick us up for dinner, but Mom said she'd like to walk.

Great, we'll probably get lost. We aren't the best with directions. Neither of us was born with an internal compass.

I claimed the loft bedroom. When I stretched out for a nap, the mattress felt like it was packed with straw. Either that or arrow-tipped twigs.

Tricked

Before we'd left home, Mom had hinted that we'd be helping Molly and Fiona prepare MacKensie Manor to be a working farm for tourists, where people could step through time and into the life of a medieval Scottish family.

I should've asked for precise details.

I figured we'd at least be staying in the castle.

I wonder if Mom knew that we'd be staying at a cottage with no electricity.

Probably. It's easy to agree to things while sitting in a room with five electrical outlets.

Now that I'm here, I'm really wondering, who would go to a working farm for a vacation?

People should go to the beach for vacations.

I should be at the beach checking out guys, or at the mall buying clothes . . . and checking out guys.

"I talked to your principal," Mom said, "and you can use the hours here as part of your hundred hours of required community service for graduation."

I snapped my pinky knuckle, a nasty habit I'd picked up in middle school. I do it when I feel helpless.

I guess helping here might be better than emptying bedpans at the local nursing home. But still, someone should've asked me. I'm sixteen, and I have a voice. When will Mom let me grow up? Someday I'll go on vacation where I want and with whom I want to go with . . . and it won't be Mom!

Home Sweet … Cottage

Our cottage has to be the worst one on MacKensie Land. Or maybe it's the best—and if that's the case, then this farm needs some serious help to become a quality tourist trap.

There are candles and oil lamps all around, so when the sun goes down, at least we still have light—even if it is a dim, creepy, stinky light.

There are two rooms downstairs. The dining, cooking, and living areas are all one big room. Mom has a small bedroom at the north end, and I'm in the loft. The "kitchen" is nothing more than a sink with a water pump and a super-old fireplace. It's the biggest fireplace I've ever seen. I tried to stand in it and hit my head, but it's still huge.

Mom has trouble cooking on the electric stove at home, so the medieval cooking thing isn't going to go over very well. Maybe now I'll lose those extra five pounds.

Molly and Fiona did leave us a cupboard full of food. I'm not sure Mom or I can cook quality homemade meals without a microwave. Dad is the cook in the family. I'm starving already.

We do have an icebox. There's a chunk of ice in there now. I wonder how long it will last.

There's no shower. I'm going to need every facial cleanser I brought with me to keep pimples at a distance. In a week, Mom will be begging to use them. Her box of pencils, erasers, and notebooks won't keep her skin clean.

Now who made the wiser purchases? Hmmm . . . I'd say me with my plethora of facial cleansers and pimple lotions.

Roughing it

We are not a *roughing it* kind of family. We are a family who vacations at a swanky beachfront condo on the Gulf Coast. Cooking over an open fire, straw-filled mattresses, no electricity, no running water . . . We are civilized people. We need modern conveniences to survive.

Help!

Walking, 7:57 p.m.

The sun was setting, and we were walking in the middle of a foreign land.

"This is so great," Mom said. "We're staying at a cottage, in Scotland." She put her arm around me.

I rolled my eyes and cracked my left pinky knuckle. "Great," I mumbled.

"Let's go," she said, pointing her finger straight ahead like she was leading a grand Scottish expedition.

"It's getting dark . . . really dark," I said. "Maybe we should stay here and try to cook something."

"Molly told me how to get there," she said. "And it's dusk, Sami, not dark."

Okay, Molly told her how to get there. Mom couldn't find the store on the corner of our street without getting lost, even with written directions and a map. And I was not much better.

"I can see my breath," I said when we stepped outside. "We could get lost and die of hypothermia."

Mom laughed. "You're such a joker, Sami. I love going places with you."

Joker? I was being dead serious.

Did I say dead?

10 Minutes After Leaving

We were lost. Mom would not admit it, but I knew.

11 Minutes After Leaving

Lights. MacKensie Castle? A mirage?

15 Minutes After Leaving

Lights were twinkling in the far, far distance.

It was pitch-black. I couldn't see where my foot was stepping, and Mom hadn't brought any form of light. She would never have made it as a Girl Scout.

(True, I never made it past Brownies, but I'm not as hopeless as Mom.)

"We're lost, aren't we?" I asked.

"No . . . we're in the Highlands," she said.

"You're such a joker, Mom." Not.

23 Minutes After Leaving

I grabbed Mom's hand. I felt like a scared baby. It was annoying.

I'm not a momma's girl. When I turned thirteen, I turned overnight into daddy's girl. Mom and I had a typical mother-and-teenage-only-child-daughter kind of relationship—tense.

I squeezed her hand. Despite our strained relationship, she would never lead me into harm.

Our steps fell into a synchronized rhythm. Left, right, left, right, left, right.

We were making progress . . . to where? Hopefully, the twinkling lights in the distance—MacKensie Castle.

"It's really dark," I said.

"Umm-hmmm."

Something crashed to our left. We froze, right legs midstride. The sound was definitely not the type of rustle created by a tiny, furry woodland Scottish creature.

No, it had been a legitimate monster-sized detonation, shattering tree limbs and possibly rocks. A large, creepy Highland monster or goblin was stalking us, using the blackness as cover.

Our breathing was soft and shallow. We stood motionless.

A howl tore through the night. A shiver raced down my spine and my eyes began to tear. We were going to die.

We squeezed hands and ran.

Right, left, right, left, right.

I heard Mom's breathing deepen. My legs shook.

"Almost . . . there," she said, gasping for breath.

We were close enough that the gleam of the manor house's lights marked our path like flashes of lightning. Safety.

Mom jerked my hand, pulling me toward the door, but I got there first and began banging. Mom stood behind me so we were back to back. She'd stop the monster from getting me. I kept my eyes focused on the grain of the wood door. Whatever was behind us, I didn't want to see.

Fiona opened the door. The stone courtyard lit up

around us. Fiona stepped back and Mom pushed me in, slamming the door. Adrenaline pumped through my body so fast, I thought my knees would buckle.

"That was exciting," Mom said, leaning back against the door. Then she started laughing.

"Yeah." I rolled my eyes and took deep breaths. I thought I was hyperventilating. I wasn't positive.

Mom had lost her mind. I was positive.

Fiona looked back and forth between Mom and me. Great—country mouse thought I was insane, a panic-stricken nutso.

At that point, I just wanted to eat, go back to our cottage with an armed guard, lock the doors, light a fire, and sleep.

Family Meal

Molly's cooking is the best I've tasted in my life. She'd made beef stew. It was thick and clung to the home-made rolls. After eating I was so content, I wanted to rub my belly. I was warm from the inside out.

I could hear Mom, Molly, and Fiona talking, but I was too full and exhausted to participate in any conversation. I'm not even sure what they talked about, since I could barely keep my eyes open.

11 p.m.

After we ate, Molly drove us back to the cottage. My heart could not have taken another stroll in the dark with Mom.

Sleeping

Fine, now I'm wide awake. The cottage is dark, and spooky quiet. I'm writing by candlelight. The small, weak flame keeps bouncing and sputtering. I hope the nightstand doesn't catch on fire.

I'm dead certain the cottage is haunted. Did I say dead? It's not like I've seen a ghost or felt a breath of cold air on the back of my neck or anything, but I know something's watching me. It's crouched in the corner at the far end of the loft, the very corner that my weak, stinky, smoky candlelight doesn't brighten.

I keep hearing this moan, like a guy rolling on the basketball court after spraining his ankle. Or maybe like someone who's walking around carrying his decapitated head.

I'm giving myself the creeps. If I had more guts, I'd get out of bed, take the candle, and check out the gloomy corner. Not.

I like watching reality shows where people hunt ghosts and stuff, while I'm sitting safe in my room living vicariously through the television personalities.

I'm going to take a deep breath, blow out the candle, and cover my head with the blanket.

If there's something here, I don't want to see it. And if I can't see it, then it won't see me.

Right?

Day 2

Breakfast

i Miss My Snooze Button

I don't eat breakfast, unless it's a piece of toast or an English muffin that I chomp while running out the door.

I love my snooze button. It's empowering to control the short bursts of time.

We were invited to eat at the manor house, MacKensie Castle. That's its official title.

I wonder how many years it takes for a run-down pile of stone to be classified as a castle. Is there a requirement for a building to be called a castle, or could I call our house back home a castle if I wanted?

The castle is half a mile east. There are two bikes outside our cottage, but again Mom decided we'd walk.

Didn't she remember last night?

Bikes would be quicker, but I wasn't biking alone in a foreign country where I barely understand anyone.

"How did you sleep?" Mom asked.

"Fine." I didn't tell her about the ghost in the corner. I've learned not to tell Mom certain things, or they wind up in one of her novels. My private life has been scattered throughout her stories. Which sucks.

Mom doesn't understand the meaning of the word "private." My bedroom is in her latest story. I'd read all about the sloppy teen girl's room on a "to be edited" page she'd left on the dining room table. I'd immediately hung a sign on my door: NO TRESPASSING.

Mom smiled. "This is so exciting. It's the perfect way for us to experience real life in Scotland. Plus, we could spend some quality time together."

My mom's having a tough time letting me grow up. Not that she's smothering me or anything, but sometimes—well, all the time—she worries too much.

Being an only child is the worst. When you're ready to spread your wings, there are no other siblings for your parents to attach themselves to.

I'm going to have lots of kids. And I'll give them all the privacy and freedom they want.

Castle, Shmatzle

It looked different in the light of day. Of course I'd seen it last night, but my mind had been focused on escaping the clutches of the night goblin. Today was my first look at the high, moss-covered stone walls, the Gothic windows trimmed with chipped black paint, and the weeds sprouting through the cobblestones of the courtyard.

Despite the run-down appearance, I know a person has to be rich to live in a castle—even an old, dusty one in the middle of nowhere. Mom and I have hit the jackpot, spending the summer with our wealthy Scottish relatives.

So why are we stuck living in a run-down cottage with no running water or electricity? MacKensie Castle, although not fancy, has to have at least a million rooms, some with power.

Okay, I'm exaggerating about a million, but it is the largest home I've ever been in. It's not a storybook castle with archer lookouts in the turrets and a moat around the perimeter; it's more like one of those castles you see on television where royalty go to spend the summer holidays.

Molly, Mom's twin—well, almost—was standing in the front courtyard wearing a wide-brimmed straw sun hat, khaki shorts, and a red T-shirt. Her arms were elbow deep in the dirt of a giant terra-cotta pot. "Morning," she said.

Of course it would've fit into my fantasy world even more to see a hot gardener doing the planting instead of Molly.

She smiled, reminding me of a kid making mud pies. Maybe she'd given the gardener the day off so she could play in the dirt.

A minute later, Mom and Molly were finishing each other's thoughts. When Molly pulled her hands out of the dirt, Mom had already moved the bucket of clean water to the bench so it was easier for Molly to reach. Molly didn't have to say a word. Creepy.

"Let's eat," Molly said, lifting her hands out of the water. Mom grabbed a towel off the stone bench and handed it to her.

"How'd ye sleep, Sami?" Molly asked.

"Good," I lied.

Where was Fiona?

She has electricity, so she was probably still hitting snooze on her alarm clock.

Always Judge a Book by its Cover

On the inside, MacKensie Castle looks like a mad scientist's lab . . . after he's tried unsuccessfully to split a zillion atoms at once.

Fiona and Molly live in five rooms: two bedrooms, the kitchen, the bathroom, and the living room. That's as far as my nosing around got me before Mom and Molly called from the kitchen. They were covered in flour, and breakfast was served. Fiona came out of her bedroom and joined us.

After breakfast, which consisted of eggs, sausage, and scones, Molly and Fiona gave us a quick tour of the rest of the castle. There were at least thirty rooms. Most were empty and had cobwebs in the corners. The few pieces of furniture were covered with dusty white sheets.

"This is the ballroom," said Molly.

Once upon a time, a long time ago, this room must have been awesome. Now it was dark, musty, and unused.

Three crystal chandeliers hung from the ceiling, each wrapped in thick, dust-covered plastic. The far wall was a sheet of floor-to-ceiling stained glass, with huge French doors; one was propped open. Through the gap I could see the stone-spindled railing of a patio.

The draft from the windows would explain the need for the monster fireplace in the center of the north wall, which made the one Mom and I had at our cottage look like a kiddies' first fire pit.

"There's a garden through the glass doors," said Fiona.

Mom was quiet. I could tell by the look on her face that she was taking mental notes. This room was transforming in her mind into descriptive words that would be included in her next novel.

I asked why they didn't use that part of the house.

"Before my husband, Angus, died," said Molly, "he'd begun the necessary restorations. We haven't had the funds to complete the process."

"We do a little at a time," said Fiona, "but we've a farm to tend also."

I'm not great with budgets, but I bet it would cost millions to restore this castle.

Dad would call MacKensie Castle a money pit.

I'd agree.

We walked back into the kitchen. Our Scottish relatives weren't rich, at least not spend-their-money-on-stupid-rich-people-kind-of-things rich.

"I'll make some tea," said Fiona.

"Molly, you tell us what we need to do," said Mom.

"Aye," said Molly. "We've a list."

No Joke: We've a List

A list should never exceed ten items. That seems fair. Ten is a good even number—not insurmountable, but still above the level of lazy.

Molly's list is snapped into a three-ring binder and categorized according to location. There are sections marked Castle, Cottages, Barns, and Pastures. Then, as if that's not crazy overorganized enough, each section is sorted by urgency and cost.

Mom can't organize a grocery list. I saw the envy in her eyes when she looked at Molly's to-do binder. This could be bad for me.

I bent my left pinky finger, pushing it down with my thumb and cracking the knuckle. I wanted to say something to Mom—something like *Don't even think about it*—but I didn't want to be too obvious, so I kept quiet and hoped she'd just admire Molly's organization and not try it at home on me.

Molly and Fiona coordinated work details before our arrival. Mom and Molly will work construction duty around the castle. Molly's been reading up on power tools. Mom gets confused with the Weed-wacker . . . so that should be good.

Fiona and I will be the farmers. There's a whole binder on that alone. I don't know anything about farming, and if I have to wear rubber waders that go up to my hips, like Fiona's stylish pair, just lock me up and throw away the key.

The Goal:
Bring in Unsuspecting Tourists and Get Them to Work Your Land for You

Molly and Fiona are insane. They're hoping to draw in the crazies who participate in reenactments and stuff. I know about a huge Renaissance festival in Holly, Michigan, every fall. I've never been, but my

English teacher, Mrs. Conklin, talked about it like it was the greatest event in the history of the world; then again, she dressed like Juliet when we read *Romeo and Juliet*. It was hard paying attention to the theme—love kills—when we were seeing parts of our teacher's anatomy that no student should see.

Back to the MacKensies' evil plan of visitor manipulation . . .

First, MacKensie Manor is working with the Society for Creative Anachronism to turn the farm into an authentic medieval reenactment place.

There has to be some basic information I'm missing, because I think people have to seriously have no life to come here and live like medieval farmers.

"Every guest will represent and play a role in the running of the farm," said Molly.

Fiona nodded. "They'll all have gardens to tend, which will be a source of the family's food. We can't feed everyone."

Great. Let's write Warning: Could Die of Starvation on the brochure.

"We've thought about the popularity of reality shows," said Molly. "People want to escape reality, live a life they would obviously never experience, but do it safely. We'll give them that."

Escape to medieval Scotland . . . I don't think so. Escape to the mall with a million dollars . . . YES.

"Advertising?" Mom asked.

"We're addressing that," Molly said. "We'll rely mainly on the Internet, linking to sites about medieval life, but we're also using the Society and relying heavily on word of mouth."

"The four cottages will each house one family," said Fiona, "or a group of six. We'll provide two sets of clothing for each participant that are authentic to the Highland medieval style."

Molly piped in. "We'll set up one of the cottages for a baker, and we'll have a blacksmith's forge built. We also need to have an area set up for dyeing wool."

"We're having a festival in five weeks," Fiona added.

"It's a yearly event in the village of Beauly," explained Molly. "We plan on having almost everything in place by then. People in the SCA visit the fair every summer."

Mom nodded.

Fiona sighed. "Mum's had it tagged on every post from here to Inverness since spring."

"Yeah, I bet *everyone* will come," I mumbled.

"Yes," Molly agreed.

Oh brother! I didn't bother saying that I was being sarcastic.

Clan War

Mom, Molly, and Fiona continued talking about the festival. The kitchen started to freak me out. I swear I could hear a voice behind the east door, which I knew led to the cellar.

I focused on the murmuring behind the door. What was it? Geez, what if they had a man locked in the basement?

I looked at everyone. Fiona smirked at me, but Mom and Molly kept talking like nothing was going on.

Didn't anyone else hear it?

The moaning spooked me out.

Maybe the cellar was the MacKensie family crypt.

"McClintoggs are pure evil," Fiona said.

"Pure evil" brought me back. The moaning was bad, but pure evil—now, that was something I had to focus on.

Fiona kept talking. "Their land runs along the

western edge of ours. They're cursed and place evil spells on anyone who comes in contact with them."

Molly laughed. "Dinnae be so dramatic, Fiona."

"I'm not," said Fiona. "And ye know it."

Molly looked at Mom. " 'Tis a history of bad blood between our two clans." She looked back at Fiona. "A rivalry that's long past, Fiona. Robert McClintogg is a good man."

"Why is there a rivalry?" I asked.

Fiona raised her hands like she was getting ready to explode into a tantrum, but Molly stopped her.

"My husband, Angus, borrowed money from a McClintogg," said Molly.

"Why?"

"Gambling!" shouted Fiona, looking at Molly. "He took back what the McClintoggs owed us after years of thieving our sheep and cattle. He didna borrow it."

Molly shook her head. "The lands of McClintogg and MacKensie used to be one. Which clan was the original owner has been debated for over a century."

" 'Tis ours," said Fiona.

"Aye now, *our* portion is." Molly looked at Mom. "I'm afraid Fiona has a touch of the clan war in her."

A touch . . . ha! Note to self: Never mention the name McClintogg to Fiona.

"Fiona's great-great-grandfather won the land in a

35

card game from a McClintogg," said Molly. "We needed money. The bank wouldn't loan us any, so Angus went to the McClintoggs."

"And made a deal with the devil," said Fiona. "McClintoggs have Satan's own blood running in their veins."

Holy crap. This girl had serious problems.

" 'Tis enough," said Molly, raising her voice. "A feud that started over a hundred years ago and is over. Dinnae try to bring it back, Fiona. I'll not have ye speaking hatred toward anyone."

Fiona didn't say anything else. We finished our tea in tense silence—except for the moaning coming from the basement, but apparently I was the only one who heard that.

These people were insane. Medieval reenactments, clan wars, family crypts in the basement, blood of Satan. . . . What had Mom gotten us into?

And more importantly, how did we get out?

Fiona

Fiona has multiple personalities.

Granted, I've never met anyone with this particular mental condition, but she has it. As soon as Molly told her to stop talking about the McClintoggs, Fiona fumed and then became the typical happy farm girl.

But I'm not going to risk being on the receiving end of her nutso rage.

She needs therapy, or a manicure, or something.

The Barn

The barn is made of the same stone as our cottage, but it's bigger and has electricity. It doesn't have a hip roof like I'd see back home in Michigan, but distinct peaks, the higher of the two sloping down over what looks like an addition.

"We have both Blackface and Cheviot breeds," said Fiona.

I nodded like I knew what she meant.

Fiona rolled her eyes. "Sheep. They're breeds of sheep."

What self-respecting teenage girl knows about sheep breeds?

She pulled the heavy door to the side. "They can survive and breed in the hills with nothing from us."

Valuable information, since that meant I wouldn't be expected to feed them.

Fiona latched the door to hold it open. "Do ye even know what a sheep looks like, or are ye too busy spending your money on their fancy wool?"

She was insulting me?

Personality three emerges.

"Yeah, I know what sheep are."

"Have ye ever seen one outside a petting zoo?"

"Ummm . . . no."

11:00 a.m.

Swept the barn. If sheep lived in the hills, why did they need a clean barn?

2:30 p.m.

Mom and Molly brought us tuna salad sandwiches. I didn't know they ate American food here.

I was filthy, and cobwebs were sticking to my sweaty skin.

I hate cobwebs. I hate sweat.

I felt like there were creepy crawlies in my hair.

She's Stuck in the Nineties

Pop music. Too nineties for me.

But the Backstreet Boys and ★NSYNC are okay boy bands to accompany sweeping brooms.

Fiona had the whole "Bye, Bye, Bye" dance down—yet another wacky personality.

Yeah, okay, I did the dance too. I mean, I was sweeping a barn, so why not?

I would never, not even under medieval torture, publicly admit to enjoying the dancing. But I did.

When the song ended, Fiona and I were laughing so hard we both had tears in our eyes.

The dancelike stomp moves really released some stress. However, my pop music preferences stay in my past—my elementary years. I've grown up and am much more mature in my musical tastes. I won't allow anything but rock to be downloaded onto my iPod. I'm not picky, though. I'm as big a fan of the retro eighties hair bands as I am of Nickelback.

My iPod is dead, and I didn't think to bring any way to charge it, so I guess I'm stuck in the nineties with Fiona.

Bye, bye, bye.

Blisters

I have a monster blister on the palm of my left hand. I should've worn gloves when I swept the barn. Who knew?

Mom said I should pop the blister, stop my whining, and go to bed.

Yeah, well, she doesn't have any blisters. You

don't get blisters from planting frilly flowers around the castle.

I hope the flowers live. Mom kills flowers. She's like the Black Death of horticulture.

Ghost in the Corner of My Loft

Thumping and heavy breathing in the corner. Can't sleep.

Day 3

Morning

According to the chore list, this week Fiona and I will be working our way through two of the four rustic cottages on the property.

Rustic? More rustic than the one Mom and I are living in? Like it could get more Middle Ages than having to boil water to take a sponge bath.

When Fiona picked me up, her hair was still wet from her shower. Never thought I'd be envious of shampoo, conditioner, a loofah, and running water, but I was.

Mom and I showered in the castle last night. Showers would have to be an evening ritual because I wasn't walking through the cold morning air, in my pajamas, to take a shower.

My manicure is a mess. Luckily I brought my own polish. If Fiona's taste in nail polish is like her taste in music, she probably has tons of hot pink.

I'll fix my nails with some black or deep purple tonight. That will suit my mood.

Cottages

It turns out that Mom and I are staying in the nicest of the four cottages at MacKensie Manor. I know that's difficult to believe, but it's true.

Fiona drove me to the cottage farthest from the

castle. I sat on the back of the four-wheeler holding a bucket of cleaning supplies in one hand, two brooms and a mop in the other.

You know, people do break their arms in accidents riding on these things.

Fiona, sensing my fear like a dog smelling raw meat, drove over the pastures like some crazed Highland witch. I must admit that once I relaxed, I enjoyed it.

The ride couldn't have taken more than twenty minutes. By the time we reached our destination, my palms were imprinted with the markings of the mop handles, and I couldn't wipe the smile off my face.

Fiona cut the engine and looked over her shoulder at me. "I love driving," she said, climbing down.

I nodded.

"What's wrong, Sami? Ye look like death."

My stomach had not gotten the message that I was having fun.

"Are ye sick?"

I hiccupped, tasting traces of vomit on the back of my tongue. I hate the fact that I have a weak stomach. Mom and Dad call it motion sickness. I call it: I'm a big fat baby.

"Why don't ye lie in the grass for a bit? That'll make ye feel better."

I climbed off the four-wheeler and plopped down on the lawn, taking deep breaths.

"Just rest for a bit," she said. "Some people cannae handle riding. Maybe ye'll get used to it. Will ye be okay?"

I closed my eyes and nodded, willing the sky to stop spinning.

"Come in when ye feel up to it," she said.

Hot Scot

Sprawled out on the grass, trying to regain my focus, I had my first look at a McClintogg—Adan McClintogg.

He didn't look like the Son of the Evil One; his genes were too good. The earth had settled around me, so my vision was fine.

He was riding a horse, kind of a squatty, muscular horse. I guess it was one of those Highland ponies I'd read about online.

Not that horses are important when I'm staring at the best-looking guy in the world.

He was so hot, the temperature within a five-mile radius increased at least ten degrees.

Maybe I was having some kind of a weird teenage hot flash. He was so handsome, my brain forgot about my queasy stomach.

He was riding beside a fence of piled stone about twenty feet behind the cottage. Gorgeousness radiated off him so strongly I could smell it from where I sat. Then I sneezed.

Crap. Was I allergic to him?

Fiona walked out the door, her attention focused on the rider and his horse. He waved. She glared.

"Fiona MacKensie!" he shouted. "What are ye doin' in that run-down cottage?"

"Get off my land, Adan McClintogg!" she shouted.

Mrs. Conklin's English lessons on *Romeo and Juliet* flashed through my brain—love kills, especially when the two families hate each other.

Well, this sucked.

I looked at Adan, then at Fiona, then back at Adan. I hoped she didn't kill him.

He pulled on the reins, stopping his horse. "I'm on my land, Fiona."

"No, 'tis mine."

"Aye, but for how much longer?"

He had the hottest voice I'd ever heard, all confident and accented. But by now he should have

45

learned to read Fiona's facial expressions. He was sitting on his horse, very near to enforcer-personality Fiona.

"We've a year to pay you, McClintogg."

"Aye." He waved to me and rode away.

"Wow." I sneezed again, stood, and walked toward Fiona.

"Adan McClintogg is an arrogant noble, a worthless man, the heir of all McClintogg Land."

"You have to pay him within the year?"

She turned and looked at me. I think she had tears in her eyes. "Before my dad died, he'd borrowed money from the McClintoggs. We've a year left to pay, or they take our farm."

"Wait," I said. "You hate the McClintoggs because you owe them money?"

"Auch, nay, I hate them because they're McClintoggs."

Clan Wars

I told Mom about the incident with Adan.

She said, "Fiona seems to be having issues dealing

with the death of her father. She wants to find some-one or something to blame it on."

"And she's picked the McClintoggs?" I said.

"Yes, and now the term of the loan is almost up, and Molly has to get the farm out of debt."

"Or the McClintoggs will take it back?"

"Yes. Molly says the McClintoggs have been wait-ing patiently. They believe the land is rightfully theirs." She sighed. "Were you not listening to anything Molly said the other day?"

"So you've brought me into a full-blown Scottish clan war, Mom? Do you have any idea how dangerous this could be? I didn't even buy any plaid before we came."

Mom looked irritated and confused. "What does your buying plaid have to do with this?" She threw a small log on the fire. She'd finished her work in the castle garden today determined to cook a quiet meal for the two of us at our cottage. "Kind of exciting, don't you think?"

"What?" I asked. "Cooking over a fire, getting blisters, the ghost in the corner of my room, or possi-bly getting killed by some lunatic rival clan member?"

Mom laughed. "Ghost?"

"Never mind."

Ghost is Making Noises
in the Corner of the Loft

Tonight my loft ghost began to thump gently on either the wall or the floor. I wish he'd leave me alone and go haunt downstairs in Mom's room.

Day 4

Fiona

Her light hair and blue eyes don't fool me. She's not a sweet, innocent girl. She's nefarious. That's a cool word—sounds wicked rolling off the tongue.

Today we worked on the second cottage, cleaning and making a list of larger repairs for our moms.

I asked, "Is the castle haunted?"

"Aye," Fiona replied.

That did not make me feel better about my loft ghost.

"I think my loft is haunted," I said.

"Aye," she said. "It's said that's where Samuel Logan hanged himself in the seventeen hundreds sometime."

I stood in the middle of the main room. Fiona moved to the windows and began washing them.

Are all Scottish people crazy? Clan wars are not normal; ghosts are not normal. How could she wash windows? What if there was a ghost here now? A chill raced down my spine.

"Why don't you have them exorcised or something?"

She didn't turn. "Why would we do that, then?"

"Why? Are you serious?"

"Aye, why cause them any more grief than they've already given themselves?"

"What if something happens?"

She stopped scrubbing. "Like what? They can't harm ye, Sami . . . they're dead."

"What about the local priest?" I asked. We were all Catholic. The Catholic Church does not approve of loose spirits. The Father could talk some sense into her. There were priests specially trained to remove

49

wandering souls and send them home . . . wherever that might be.

"Father Stanley," she said. "Aye, he's a good man and loves a good bit of ghost hunting." She dipped her rag into the bucket of soapy water.

"Priests aren't supposed to like ghosts," I said. "They're supposed to get rid of them."

Fiona squeezed the rag and looked at me for a minute. "Why would Father Stanley be wantin' to get rid of Samuel?"

"He's a ghost," I said.

"Aye, and that's no reason to be exorcising him." She looked at me like I was the nutso one.

I grabbed my bucket of soapy water and sponge. "It's not normal, Fiona," I said, moving as far away from her as I could, which wasn't very far considering this cottage didn't have a loft.

Ghosts probably loved her.

Samuel Logan

I was alone in the cottage. Mom hadn't returned from her work detail with Molly, and Fiona had dropped me off about twenty minutes ago.

I was sitting at the table when I felt the cold breath on the back of my neck. The hair on my arms rose. I had to work to swallow. I forced myself not to run.

"Sam," a voice whispered, bouncing from one wall to another.

I took a breath. "What?" I was not sure I'd said the word aloud. I looked around the room. I was alone. "What?"

"I am Samuel," the bodiless voice said.

I leaned back in the chair so I was balancing on the two back legs. "Who?"

"Samuel Logan. Are ye dim-witted, lass?"

A breeze moved over my thighs. I jerked, and the chair flung out from under me. My bottom hit the wood floor. "Knock it off!" I shouted.

The cup I'd been drinking water out of flew off the table.

"What the heck?" I said, standing.

"Ye said knock it off."

My butt hurt, my water was all over the floor, and I was carrying on a conversation with a dumb guy-ghost named Samuel Logan. "What do you want?"

"I think I'm a spirit," he said.

"Duh."

"I dinnae understand the word 'duh.' "

I shook my head. "Never mind."

I stood there silent. I didn't know what to say to a ghost.

The quiet lasted so long I thought he'd gone. I sighed and sat down.

"What?" Samuel said.

I jumped up and cracked my pinky knuckle. "What do you want?" I asked. Geez, was he just going to stand around and never leave? That was creepy.

"I dinnae know," he said.

"Huh?"

"Huh. I dinnae—"

". . . know what that means," I finished. "Why are you here?"

"I dinnae know. Lass, how many times do I need to tell ye?"

Great. He was insulting me. "I can't see you," I said.

"Aye, right . . . ye cannae see me? 'Tis not good. I can see you," he said.

"That's because I'm alive." He was trying my patience.

"Aye. I think I'm dead."

"You think?" Samuel Logan wasn't a very confident ghost.

The house became quiet again. I called Samuel's name three times, but he didn't answer. I have no idea where he went. Maybe he exorcised himself.

I'm keeping this encounter to myself. If I tell Mom, she'll quiz me, digging for details so she can write a paranormal scene.

Day 5

Cows

A farm with sheep in the hills taking care of themselves would be an okay farm by me. But, no, as it turns out, the MacKensies also have a couple of dairy cows. I've been given charge of one while Fiona takes care of the other.

Fiona's cow is named Sugar because she is sweet and gentle. Mine is named Bessie, daughter of Beelzebub. Fiona calls her Bessie; I added the Beelzebub because it fits her distressed, evil personality. She's probably possessed by one of the nasty ghosts Fiona's so fond of keeping around. Or maybe she's a McClintogg cow.

The disaster began with Fiona handing me a bucket, pointing to Bessie, and giving the command to milk her. *Okay.* I hadn't done or said anything that would make her believe I had any history of milking a cow. I don't like looking stupid, though, so I watched her for a minute, memorizing her every move. If she could do it, I could. I don't have a brother or sister, so I'd never experienced sibling rivalry until then. And since Fiona is just a distant relative, maybe it's a good thing I'm an only child.

I put the three-legged stool at Bessie's right side, sat down, and cleaned the udder with the wet rag. Then I closed my eyes, reached out, and grabbed a teat. It felt like dried rubber.

I took a deep breath, opened my eyes, and pulled. Milk streamed out and soaked onto the straw-covered ground.

Dang . . . I forgot the bucket.

I placed the bucket under the udder and began pulling and milking. The bucket was filling. That was easy. I figured I'd be out-milking Fiona in another five minutes.

I moved on to another teat and pulled. I still had the other side to finish. From my peripheral vision, I saw Fiona moving around Sugar, carrying her bucket and stool.

Dang. *Pull faster, Sami.*

I'd get quicker and become Queen Milkmaid.

Okay. I needed to focus.

Get a grip, Sami.

The teat was dry. I stood. I could not walk in front of Bessie because her nose was pressed into a wad of hay hanging on the wall. I had to go behind her. I hated walking behind big animals.

What if she kicked me?

I closed my eyes and in one big hop-step was past her backside.

Confident that I understood the milking process, *I had become one with the cow,* I sat and grabbed another teat. Bessie seemed more uncomfortable with me on this side. My heart was racing. The more timid I became, the more she twitched.

Her tail constantly whacked me in the face like I

was some annoying cow-milk fly. Then, with one well-aimed crack, Bessie's tail flew into my open mouth. Long cow hair . . . gross. There was dried brown stuff on it. I spit. Disgusting.

I don't want to know.

Bessie kicked the bucket over—twice.

I lost most of the milk. The second time, I fell off the stool trying to stop the tipping bucket, and my butt landed in a wet puddle that I hoped was spilled milk. I had straw in my tennis shoes, cow hair in my mouth, and milk caked on the butt of my Abercrombie jeans.

Fiona laughed. I didn't have to turn and look at her. I could picture her nose crinkled into that annoying expression she gets before she begins to snort-laugh.

There was nothing funny about this. I was determined to finish milking—although I would've loved to let Bessie's milk glands swell and shrivel, or whatever happens to a cow when she's not milked.

In the end, Fiona's bucket was filled to the top. Mine wasn't. She'd won this round.

Fiona smiled. "Now we churn it into butter."

Oh . . . bring it on.

My Arms Are Falling Off

Churning butter is a punishment that should only be given to the most hardened criminals. Fiona says it's one of the jobs that people vacationing here will be able to perform.

Right. You'd have to pay *them* to stay here.

Molly and Fiona's vision of saving MacKensie Manor by turning it into a working farm/vacation-reenactment destination is the world's worst money-making scheme.

Day 6

Mom's in Writer Mode

She's sitting at the table, her journal open in front of her, writing notes and drawing sketches.

Mom always gets quiet when she's putting new elements of a story together. Plus, the new journal is a telltale clue. Each story gets its own special notebook.

Mom has boxes of journals—pages and pages of plots, characters, settings, and research. They're stored in a corner of the attic. They only make it to that sacred storage location if the stories have been published. The living room and her bedroom are full of the journals she's keeping on unpublished works.

She hasn't talked to me about any of her stories for two years, probably because the last time she did, I told her that romances were stupid, and that she should try writing a mystery. Smart people buy mysteries, I said. She told me I was wrong and hasn't talked to me about a story since.

I kind of miss it.

From what I remember, Mom has some pretty cool women in her stories. You know, the tough, I-am-so-confident-I-can-handle-anything type. Most of them have really cool careers, too. There was an astronaut, a mortician, an archaeologist . . .

Any one of Mom's heroines would know how to cook using a fire.

I wish Mom did.

I'm taking a lamp upstairs tonight. The glass globe

is dark and burned from the flame, but I'm hoping it will give off more light than my stubby, stinky candle.

I'm going to try to talk to ghost Samuel.

My curiosity has overridden my fear. I want to know what he wants. He has to be the ghost in my loft.

Day 7

Morning

Samuel did not come back. I sat up half the night waiting, and even called his name a couple of times.

He's so rude.

My mind keeps repeating the encounter with him. I can't get rid of his voice. I have to know what's what, once and for all.

When Am i Going to See Anything in the Highlands Besides MacKensie Manor?

5:00 p.m.

I just got back from a bike ride. I thought it would be sweet. I haven't ridden since middle school because that's when it became uncool. The cool kids drove to school, or rode with someone who drove.

I was pedaling down a dirt road—more like a path, really. I was kind of lost, but I knew I was still on MacKensie Land.

There, riding his squatty horse toward me, was Adan McClintogg.

I took a deep breath. Geez, he's so hot. The palms of my hands began sweating.

Wet palms do not grip metal handlebars too well. Add to that the rock that appeared in the path of my front tire, and I was in the middle of the single most embarrassing event of my life to date.

The front tire hit the rock, jerking my hands off the handlebars. My sweaty palms couldn't get a grip on the slick metal and the bike launched forward like some circus sideshow stunt in which I was starring as the idiot clown.

I felt my bottom rise from the seat, and my feet instinctively kicked out to the sides. I gave up trying to grip the handlebars.

For a second, time stopped, and I knew I looked like some deranged X-Games wannabe. I felt myself blush even though I knew the timing was stupid. Adrenaline and shyness make a dumb combination.

The bike landed with a crash a full second before my body smacked the ground beside it.

I was breathing short and fast, like when you get hit in the stomach with a ball. I was lying on my back, although I wasn't sure how I'd landed in that position. I clearly remember heading toward the ground face-first.

I closed my eyes and concentrated on breathing. A wet, snotty nose touched my cheek. I opened my eyes and looked into the huge nostrils of Adan's horse. The beast stuck its nose against my neck and pushed.

I swatted at it. "Sick," I cried.

I heard the crunch of shoes before I saw Adan's boots. It was my first up-close look at the hot Scot. I don't think I'd hit my head, but a head injury was the only explanation I had for my seeing the light that radiated around him — or maybe it was the way his body blocked the sunlight, or maybe he was a Scottish god.

"Are ye injured?" he asked.

Oh yeah, could you give me CPR or something? I thought.

As he squatted beside me, the sun, which had been hidden behind him, blinded me. He was real.

I was having trouble breathing, and now I was seeing red dots.

"Can ye speak, lass?"

"Yes." I was hurt, not stupid.

"Did ye break anything?"

"I don't know."

"Let me check before ye move." He began pressing his fingers along my legs, starting at my ankles. He stopped at my thighs, winked, and moved his fingers up to check my ribs.

Apparently nothing was broken because he stood and said, "Knocked the wind out of ye."

"Yeah." I sat up, confident in his medical assessment. I wished I had broken something. Then I wouldn't have felt so stupid.

"I'm Adan McClintogg," he said, holding his hand out and helping me to my feet.

"I'm Sami Ames."

"The American guest staying with the MacKensies?"

"Yeah."

"Let me move the bike, and I'll put ye on the horse and give ye a ride home."

I looked at the bike. "I'm fine. I'll just ride . . ." The front tire was bent almost in half.

". . . the horse home," he said, and laughed.

Riding

We stood next to Adan's horse. "Have ye ridden before?" he asked.

"Yeah," I said, not wanting to sound dumb. I already looked like some bike-riding moron. Besides, it was true—I had ridden before, when I was seven, at the local fair's pony ride.

Adan figured out my lie within two seconds. I gave myself away when I didn't know exactly how to get on. At the fair, my dad had picked me up and placed me in the saddle.

Adan looked from the horse to me and back. "You're hurt. Let me help you." He winked again.

I smiled. He'd given me a way out. It was so romantic. "Okay," I whispered.

He lifted me, making me feel small for the first time in my teen life. Being almost six feet tall and not model skinny, I haven't felt tiny in years. I've wondered where I'd find a guy strong enough to carry me over the threshold on my wedding night.

He sat me in the saddle and swung up behind me, wrapping his left arm around my waist and grabbing the reins with his right hand.

My stomach did a weird flop. I'd die if I threw up.

His knees pressed into the outsides of my thighs as he gently squeezed with his heels against the horse's flanks, urging him forward. Holy cow . . . or holy horse.

Adan leaned forward and spoke in my ear. "Are ye enjoying your stay?"

I tried to think but was having a hard time concentrating. He was too close. I really hope Mom writes scenes like these in her romance novels. This is great material. I should let her know.

"Yeah," I said.

"Trying to help save MacKensie Castle and land?"

"Yeah."

He smelled like outside—how dorky a thought is that? Sounds like a rotten line in a bad romance movie.

He made a clicking sound, and the horse began to jog. I'm sure there's some fancy riding term for the pace, but I don't know it. All I know is, it was a lot faster than the pony ride at the fair.

I loved it: the speed, the wind in my face. It was like riding a bike, but without the work and on top of a sweaty beast instead of a lifeless metal frame. Plus, I didn't get sick to my stomach.

And I bet the horse wouldn't stumble over a small rock in the road.

Adan pulled the horse to a stop about half a mile from MacKensie Castle. "You'll have to walk from here. I'm not welcome."

"But—"

" 'Tis fine, Sami Ames," he said, jumping down and offering me his hand. "You go help save MacKensie Manor." He climbed back on his horse. "Would ye care if I called on ye, Sami?"

"I don't have a phone."

He laughed. "Auch, you're a funny one. I mean, may I come and visit ye and perhaps take ye out a time or two?"

"Oh," I said. "Umm . . . yeah." I smiled. He wanted to go on a date with me. YES!

"Aye, good, then," he said, and rode off into the sunset.

That sounds hokey, but he really was riding toward the setting sun.

Day 8

Hot List

Green eyes: Love a guy with

green eyes.

Black hair: Small curls at end

and kind of shaggy-sexy.

Nice hands: Not girly

hands—hot.

Tall: I'm too tall for short guys.

Voice: When he says things

like "aye," I get all tingly.

Mackensies Really Hate McClintoggs. And I'm Not Fooling.

Fiona *hates* McClintoggs.

"Why?" I asked at breakfast, still having trouble with the whole clan war thing.

"Because they want our land and will stop at nothing to get it," she said.

"Like what?" I asked.

She shook her head like I was the one with the mental condition, and walked away.

I think Fiona and I could be friends, if she had better style and stopped trashing Adan. She's ruining my whole from-a-distance-really-infatuated-I-want-to-live-in-your-castle Adan thing.

Day 9

Darn Ghost

Samuel Logan is ticking me off.

It's not enough that he won't talk to me and hides in the dark making thumping noises, but now he's throwing things at me. There were feathers all over the bed when I woke up this morning.

Mom says my pillow probably ripped or something, but I checked all the seams and none of them were torn. Plus, it was still fluffy.

It was Samuel.

What is his problem? What does he want from me?

It'll take more than your little feather boo to scare me, Samuel.

I think it's time for a paranormal investigation.

I wonder if I can get Fiona to help me. With all her "ghosts are welcome" talk, I bet she'd be all for it.

It'd be something we could do together besides clean.

Maybe we'd become friends.

Or at least I could become friends with one of her nutso personalities.

The sticking point is, I don't know how to hunt ghosts, or what to do when I hear from Samuel again.

Day 10

i Want a Favorite Spot

Today Fiona took me to what she calls her favorite spot.

She'd packed a lunch of peanut butter, sugar, and apple sandwiches. They were so good.

I rode on the back of the four-wheeler. I'm used to her driving now and have learned to lean into the turns, which makes the ride more tolerable, and, I'm reluctant to admit, kind of fun.

MacKensie Manor is beautiful. Back home we live in a rural community and I see farmland every day, but here it's different. The land rolls, and when you reach the top of a hill, there are small valleys waiting below. It's like the green pastures, trees, and lakes are inviting you into their magical world.

Okay, enough of the magical mushy stuff.

We stopped and Fiona spread out a small wool blanket. "This is it," she said. "My favorite place in the world."

Do I have a favorite place in the world? Maybe the American Eagle store back home.

Fine—I'm shallow. But at least I dress well.

Friends

Fiona and I are becoming friends.

If we were in Allentown, I guess I'd take her to the mall with me. I've kind of gotten used to her personality.

Day 11

Laundry

I'm out of clean clothes. I brought this to Mom's attention, and she announced, "Laundry day," as if it was a national holiday.

Who knows, maybe it is in Scotland?

At home I'd put my dirty clothes in the laundry room and they'd appear the next day clean and folded in a laundry basket inside my bedroom door. I've always suspected that elves come in overnight and help Mom do the laundry.

Mom told me to follow her outside. In the back of our cottage is a fire pit with a large black pot hanging from a metal pyramid frame. She stood beside it and pointed. "Washing machine." Then she pointed to a clothesline. "Dryer."

Antique yard decorations were our Laundromat?

"You've got to be kidding," I said.

"Nope," she said.

Whatever.

We live in the modern world, and Mom's pretending that we've traveled through some stupid time warp. I'm being pretty mature about the whole no Internet, no cell phone, no electricity, and no hot water thing, but this is dumb.

"Can't you just wash it at the castle?" I asked.

Mom shook her head. "We're here to help set up a program for tourists. Doing laundry with a washboard and cauldron full of boiling water will be part of the experience."

"But we're not tourists. We're family," I said. "No way will people pay to do this."

"Yes they will," Mom said. "People are willing to pay big money to get away from it all and go back to simpler things."

"Simple is sending your laundry out to be done," I said, "not doing it like some medieval peasant."

"Don't be such a spoilsport. Bring over some wood from the pile. I'll get some water."

I felt like a witch brewing a wicked potion as I moved the large wooden paddle in slow circles around the black pot full of boiling water and dirty laundry. I just needed to add some eye of newt and I'd have a truly menacing concoction.

I've always known that someday I'd have to learn to do laundry. I never thought it'd be like this.

By the time the fire was going strong and the water was boiling, Mom and I had three huge piles of clothes in different areas. Whites were sitting closest to the pot. Mom says it's best to wash those first while the water is cleanest. Then lights and finally darks.

Mom brought a big metal tub out and filled it with cold water. "Rinse," she said.

Neither the pot nor the tub could hold more than five or six things at a time. I stirred in the first batch of undergarments. This would not be good for my new lacy push-up bra. I held my breath and circled the paddle slowly—gentle cycle.

That was laundry day—a day of torture, burned fingers, gross-smelling homemade soap, and quality time with Mom.

Ruined My Favorite Jeans

All the laundry is washed and hanging to dry.

I ruined my favorite pair of jeans. There's a hole in the left knee from the ancient washboard. It's not one of those cool store-bought rips, either. It looks like I got caught in a meat grinder. Guess they're my chore pants now.

My T-shirts look like boards hanging from the line. They're all stiff. Even my underwear is stiff.

That homemade soap is disgusting. I don't even want to know what's in it, but I'm sure it's not fabric softener.

Day 12

Fiona Is Going to Be My Ghost-hunting Partner

Fiona has agreed to help hunt the ghost of Samuel Logan. She says she wants to talk to him.

I'm not sure she's on the same wavelength as I am with the ghost-hunting stuff. I want Samuel gone, and Fiona wants him to have tea and a paranormal conversation.

But despite being lost in nineties style, Fiona is very up-to-date in the world of technology. She has a digital camera, a video recorder, and a computer in her room. We got on the Internet and pulled information on ghost-hunting and what to do with a ghost once you make contact. I guess things work a little differently when you go and find them as opposed to them finding you.

We've educated ourselves.

What could go wrong?

Day 13

Calling Samuel Logan

Fiona came over wearing black pants and a black shirt. She looked like she was going to a poetry reading.

She brought her digital camera. I was touching technology again, but my fingers were so burned from laundry day that I had no feeling in them, so Fiona had to snap the pictures.

Besides the research online, neither of us had any experience with ghost-hunting, but we'd both read enough books and watched enough television to know what the paranormal experts say: Are you there? Show us a sign.

We could probably have used a medium. Since neither of us could communicate with the dead, we had to rely on intuition and digital photographic evidence.

I sat on the corner of my straw mattress, and Fiona sat beside me. We'd each had five cups of coffee and were armed with flashlights. Mom was down-stairs, hopefully asleep.

We waited. Silence.

"Are ye there, Sam?" Fiona whispered.

It was so quiet, she kind of scared me. "Why are you whispering?" I asked.

She shrugged. "Seems like what ye should do when speaking with the dead."

"Yeah, you wouldn't want to wake them," I said.

"No. Respect," she said.

"They're dead."

"Aye."

We waited some more. More silence.

"He's not doing anything," I said.

"Aye," Fiona said. "Maybe he's scared."

"Scared of what?" I asked. "He's the ghost."

She shrugged. "I read once that living people are like ghosts to the dead." She turned to me. "And you're not wearing black."

Ah. That made no sense.

We waited. Silence.

We waited. And fell asleep.

Day 14

8 a.m.

We need another plan to catch Samuel Logan. He's an uncooperative ghost.

321 sheep

Today we went into the hills to count sheep. Really.

Yes, I counted 321 sheep. No, I didn't fall asleep. Ha—that's a joke. Get it? Counting sheep puts people to sleep.

Day 15

Shopping

I miss shopping with my friends. I said something about malls and shopping to Fiona today, and she looked at me like I'd grown another head.

What teenage girl in her right mind doesn't understand spending a day at the mall with her girlfriends and her parents' money? I won't even go into the fact that shopping helps build budgeting skills.

Fiona says she doesn't like shopping.

Gasp!

What is her problem? A girl can't live on a sheep farm her whole life. She needs to get out there and experience the world.

Market

Fiona handled my withdrawal from shopping like a true and concerned friend.

Today she took me into the village of Beauly to shop. You can't imagine how excited I was. Are you kidding? I couldn't wait to try things on and smell new, just-hung-on-hangers clothes. Heaven.

But Beauly is a tiny village, and shopping—well, Fiona took me to a farmers' market.

The one main street was lined with booths selling farm-grown stuff. Fiona bought some vegetables; a live chicken, which we had to carry home in a crate (and I think we ate for dinner); and some herbs, purchased from an elderly man, that I think she's going to use to make Samuel Logan show himself to us. I couldn't understand what she and the old man were saying to each other, but I heard the word "spirit" in the conversation.

Walking home took about an hour, since we had to share chicken-carrying duty. Fiona talked on and on about how we'd surely see Samuel in the early hours of the morning.

Hot Adan Alert

Adan stopped by tonight. When I saw him riding his horse down the path toward our courtyard, my stomach flipped a million times.

He's so handsome.

Luckily, Fiona had gone home to get her cameras and other ghost-hunting gear, otherwise she'd probably have thrown eggs at him.

Last year in social studies, Mr. Minkton talked about Greek mythology. He told us that Eros, according to legend, was so hot that if a woman looked at him, she'd go blind. At the time, I figured that Eros had to be one heck of a hottie to make women lose their vision.

Adan is like a modern-day Eros. That's how fine he is.

He asked me to go to Loch Ness tomorrow on a date.

"To see the Loch Ness monster?" I asked.

He laughed. "Aye, if she shows herself. And for a picnic."

Mom said I could go. YES!

But I'll need my sunglasses . . . I don't want to go blind. Ha.

He's picking me up at noon.

Samuel Logan

Okay, so Fiona and I made contact with Samuel Logan. At least I think we did.

Fiona, wearing black again, came over. She made a circle of dried herbs in the corner and then did some freaky chant thing.

I didn't see or hear anything. Honest.

But as soon as Fiona finished the chant, she snapped a million still pictures and pushed Record on her video camera. She did this for about five minutes without stopping. Then she sat on the bed and flipped back through her photos, listening to the sounds. Apparently she'd been using the voice recorder also.

"There he is," she said, jumping off the bed and shoving the display in my face. "Do ye see him, Sami? Do ye?"

I looked at the screen. "No."

She sighed and pointed. "There. It's a light anomaly. Remember, that's how spirits use their energy to show themselves?"

I saw what looked like a speck of dust. But I remembered reading about that phenomenon online. "I see it."

"Aye," she said, turning the camera so she could look at the display. "And listen." She pushed a button. "This is his voice."

I really tried to hear something, but all I could catch was a sound like a gurgling wind.

She pressed the button and played it again. "Did ye hear that?"

I nodded. I wasn't really sure what she'd heard, but I didn't think I'd heard anything significant.

"Did ye hear what he said, Sami?"

I nodded again.

"What do ye think he means?"

I'd heard a gurgle, nothing ghastly, so I shrugged.

She sighed. "He didn't kill himself, didn't ye hear? I'll play it again." She pushed the button. "Mc-Clintogg," she whispered.

My skin went all goose-bump cold. "No," I said.

"Aye, Sami . . . in Sam's own voice." She looked at me for a long time, then said, "You know, you have the same name. That's why he's connecting with you."

Holy crap. Fiona was freaking me out.

"You think—"

"His words." She nodded at the camera. "There've always been rumors surrounding Sam's death," she said. "A lot of folks don't believe he'd take his own life. McClintoggs killed him."

"Fiona," I said, gulping deep breaths to calm myself. "I just want Samuel gone."

"Aye, I understand." Her eyes were huge. "But we'll have to release his soul."

I nodded. "Okay, then let's release it."

" 'Tis not that simple, Sami," she whispered. "We'll have to bring him justice, right the wrong done to him."

I wished she'd stop whispering.

"Why?"

"Didna ye pay attention at all when we researched?" she said. "He can't cross over until his soul is at rest, and as long as people think he killed himself, he'll not find peace, and he'll be trapped here forever."

"Yeesss. Trapped."

Crap. We had made contact with Samuel, and he was talking to us. Fiona and I both jumped, and her mind clicked into gear more quickly than mine. Before I fully registered that I'd just heard a spirit voice, she was snapping pictures. "Did ye hear that, Sami?"

"Yes," I said.

I'd definitely heard that.

"McClintogg," said Samuel.

"Talk to him, Sami," Fiona urged, still taking pictures.

"Why me?"

"You're his namesake," she said.

"What?" She'd lost her mind. "I don't want to talk to him."

"McClintogg!" Samuel shouted. An unlit candle fell off the nightstand. Then a burst of cold air swept over me, and I knew he'd gone. "He's left," I said.

Fiona stopped taking pictures. "Why didn't you talk to him?" she asked. "We had him where we wanted him."

"Why didn't *you* talk to him?" I shot back. "Just because his name is Samuel and mine is Samantha doesn't mean we can communicate through realms or that he's come here to talk to me."

"Aye, well, 'tis done," said Fiona. "Next time, talk."

"*You* talk."

"Tomorrow we'll go to town," she said. "We've got to find facts surrounding Samuel Logan's death."

I nodded. The sooner we solved the mystery, the sooner Samuel would be gone and I would get some rest.

"In the morning?" I asked.

"Aye," she said.

"Good." I had a date with Adan in the afternoon, but that was something I'd rather not discuss with Fiona.

Day 16

7 a.m.

I'm so tired. Thanks to ghost Samuel, and now ghost-hunter-personality Fiona, I haven't had a good night's sleep since I arrived.

Fiona slept over the past two nights, and I listened to her constant ramblings until three a.m. both times.

Samuel only made the one appearance. Apparently Fiona's too much of a talker for him.

I'd finally hit a deep sleep around 6:30. Then at the butt-crack of dawn, Fiona put a cup of hot tea under my nose, saying she wanted to get to the public records building before the crowd.

I'm not sure what public records buildings are like

in Scotland, but at home I don't think I've ever heard of one with a crowd. Fiona was acting like she was going early-bird shopping the morning after Thanksgiving.

10 a.m.

A wasted morning.

On the bright side, I got to sit in a stuffy room working some ancient microfiche machine and smelling musty old papers instead of combing the hills counting sheep.

I didn't know what Fiona expected to find on Samuel Logan. There were no CSI units in the 1700s.

According to public record, there's never even been a Samuel Logan living in this area, although we did find documentation of the birth of a Samuel Logan MacKensie. It had to be him.

The old man who supervised the records sat beside us the entire morning. His breath smelled like after-dinner mints. His name was Roland, and he said there'd been a fire in the early 1900s. Although most documents had been saved, Samuel's had not.

It's as if Samuel Logan never existed. Maybe he didn't. Maybe he's nothing more than a rumor. Maybe he was a MacKensie—but Fiona was adamant that no MacKensie had ever died by hanging. And legends around ghost Samuel clearly state he was hanged.

Maybe Samuel was the product of my overactive imagination, freaking me out in a strange environment. But Fiona had heard him too. Hadn't she?

I tried to explain my imagination theory to her. She wouldn't hear it. Well, she was quiet while I talked, and then when I paused, she said tonight we'd have to get more photographic evidence. Her obsessive personality is dominating her brain.

The Best Date of My Entire Life

Adan was on time.

I hate it when people are late. It really bugs me.

Thankfully, he didn't ride his horse. He drove up in a hot black sports car. It was sweet and made me all weak in the knees.

I could've kissed him then. I wanted to, but not on the first date. Mom's drilled that into my head since middle school. She didn't know I'd already been kissed on the playground once. No reason to let her know that Derek Price had already taught me the basics of a good lip-lock.

Back to the date.

Adan came to get me, brought Mom flowers, and opened the car door for me.

Imagine some guy in Michigan doing any of that. Not.

Then we drove to Loch Ness. Adan drives like he rides his horse, all confident, and cocky enough to increase his hotness by ten degrees.

I have to say that Loch Ness is nothing more exciting than a big lake. I live around a lot of lakes, so one more isn't all that thrilling unless I'm jet-skiing or something.

But the point of visiting Loch Ness was to see the Loch Ness monster, Nessie. We parked on a hill overlooking the lake.

"The best place to see Nessie," Adan said. "I'll get the food. You choose the spot and spread the blanket." He reached into the backseat, pulled out a dark blue plaid blanket, and passed it to me.

His hand touched mine, and he held it there a little longer than necessary.

Goose bumps. For real.

Lunch was interesting. Adan might be a rich noble and all, but he'd packed simple meat sandwiches, a jar of pickles, a bag of chips, a box of store-bought cookies, and canned lemonade. Besides the homemade bread, everything looked like it had just been taken right out of the pantry and packed in the wicker basket. Putting the whole thing together probably took five minutes, but for a guy that's pretty impressive.

Adan has probably never had to pack a lunch a day in his life. I bet he's always had a servant to do it for him. That he'd taken the time to pack lunch for me made my stomach tingle. He's so hot, and thoughtful. At least I *think* he packed it.

What would it be like to have servants? Mom always says to me, "I'm not your servant, Sami." It'd be so cool to have some, though. One to do my laundry, one to cook pancakes for every meal, one to bake me bread. Adan's bread smells so awesome—sweet and fresh.

"Do you have a cook?" I asked.

"Aye. Don't ye?"

I almost spit out my lemonade. *Yeah, my dad.* "No," I said.

It got quiet then. He probably thought I was some kind of commoner. No cook . . . really. What kind of a person doesn't have a cook? Ummm . . . me.

I tried to focus on the water and ignore the tingling that had turned to an ache in my stomach. I felt out of place. Back home I was kind of sought after by the guys. It wasn't like I had a different date every weekend, but I was the only freshman asked to the winter formal last year, so I'm far from hopeless.

The water in the lake was really blue.

It was quiet. Nothing to talk about. *I'm a peasant, living in a medieval no-electricity cottage.*

Great. I was there with dreamboat "I have a cook" Adan, and I was focusing on the color of the lake.

Adan cleared his throat. " 'Tis fine ye don't have a cook, Sami. I didna ask ye here for your family wealth."

Great. He thinks I'm a loser, and poor.

He continued. "I asked you to come with me because I wanted to show you the mystical power of my country."

Great. Now he was going all supernatural-patriotic.

"Would ye like to know the magic of the land, Sami?"

"Yes," I said. What else was I going to say? *No, Adan, don't tell me anything about your magical country.*

I turned and looked at him. I could listen to him talk about his magical country, or whatever, for days.

He smiled, and my stomach tingled again. Mom

always said if a guy gives you that weird, happy, I-want-to-throw-up feeling, it's special.

My stomach gurgled.

"Hungry?" Adan said, handing me a sandwich.

I nodded. I wasn't going to tell him that it wasn't hunger noises my stomach was making. My stomach was sending messages to my brain: Adan and I would date, he'd come to the States and we'd go to college together, we'd get married, live in his castle, and have five children.

"Do you have any brothers or sisters?" I asked.

"No."

Perfect. He'd want lots of kids too.

Maybe I was getting ahead of myself.

My stomach was going nuts, sending crazy nervous in-love signals to my brain.

I've always hated the thought of eating in front of a guy, and I hate my queasy stomach. I have only done it a couple of times. This time, however, was all I needed to know that I never want to do it again for the rest of my life. My husband will eat in a separate room.

Here's why: When I took a bite, some of the food didn't make it all the way into my mouth. There's nothing more disturbing than having a guy make eye contact when you know there's a hunk of ham hanging out of the corner of your mouth.

Every swallow sounded like I was trying to force down a boulder of meat. I wasn't sure if the romantic atmosphere had somehow heightened my sense of hearing, or if I was just now realizing what a pig I was.

I was starving, but my brain wouldn't relax enough to eat. My stomach was sick, like I wanted to vomit.

My irrational thoughts made no sense. Adan's offer of a nice, calm picnic had become more like an invitation to a twisted carnival ride gone wrong.

Somehow, amid my inner turmoil and Adan's teasing smile, I finished my sandwich.

I'm not sure what kind of meat I ate. I didn't taste a thing.

Medieval Crossbow Shooting

" 'Tis like the modern sniper rifle," said Adan, lifting a wooden crossbow out of the trunk of his car.

I nodded. I'm no expert on weapons, but I know

enough to understand the deadly killing capacity of this particular bow.

Awesome!

Adan set the bow on the ground and pulled out a stack of arrows and a round straw target. I was going to shoot a crossbow! It was a skill I'd never need, like golf, but I wanted to learn.

"Longbowmen were highly trained marksmen," he said, carrying the target to a tree and leaning it against the trunk with its face turned to us. "They were expensive to train, and it could take years to replace a dead one." He walked back to me and pointed at the bow on the ground. "A crossbow, anyone could use. It was not as effective as a longbow, but it worked."

I nodded. "Would you have used a crossbow?"

He laughed. "Auch, nay, Sami. I would have been a knight—the tank of the medieval battlefield."

"Ah, then how do you know how to fire one?" I was so pumped. My hands were itching to hold the weapon. I cracked my pinky knuckle.

He stopped and picked up the bow. "I love the history of my country," he said. "Some is magical, like Nessie, and some a matter of practical survival. The crossbow is about survival."

"In battle?"

"Aye," he said. " 'Tis necessary when laying siege

to a castle to have weaponry equal to, if not better than, your enemy's."

I nodded like I understood castle sieges. The closest I'd ever come to something like that was the one time I'd locked my parents out of my bedroom. I was twelve and angry and rather fond of slamming doors to make my point. My parents had laid siege to my bedroom by simply removing the door.

Adan picked up the bow and held it with respect. Then he started talking, but I had a hard time focusing on his words; he was speaking a foreign language. ". . . a light coat of wax on the shelf . . . string of whipcord . . . lubricate the mechanisms . . . exposed wood makes the best prods . . . split in the grain is dangerous . . . the bow irons add more weight . . ."

I watched and smiled. I was listening, but he was so hot I didn't want to tell him that I didn't have a clue what he was talking about.

"Come, I'll show you," he said, holding the firing end pointed at the ground. He placed his right foot on the back of the bowed part and pulled the string up. "Like that. Ye want to keep the string resting in the groove of your first knuckles." He held up his right hand with his fingers bent. "You won't have as much pain in your shoulders tonight if you pull keeping your elbows straight."

I raised my eyebrows. Couldn't he just load the bow for me and I'd pull the trigger? I guess that wouldn't have been very sportsperson-like.

Adan handed me the bow, and I put my foot on the back just the way he had and pulled. Nothing.

"Give it a good tug," he said.

I tried again; the string moved slightly. I'm not weak. I've taken weight-training classes for two years.

Adan stepped behind me and put his arms around me. No way was I going to tell him I was strong enough to do this, not when I was all snug in his arms.

He grabbed the string, placed his hands over mine, and helped me pull the string back and lock it behind the arrow.

My knees were weak, and I could feel my fingers tremble slightly. He kept his hands on top of mine, like a calming breath slowing my heart and my shaking.

With his arms wrapped around me, I felt like this would be as close to pure contentment as I'd ever get for the rest of my life. Never mind that I was holding one of the medieval world's deadliest weapons.

Adan raised his arms, and mine followed. "We'll aim," he whispered in my right ear, "and squeeze the trigger."

I followed the fluidity of his voice and the gentle

coaxing of the muscles in his arms and hands. Mom better write stuff like this in her romance novels.

"Now?" I asked, surprised that I could still form and speak words.

"Aye, Sami." His breath moved in and around my ear.

I pulled the trigger because the other option was to pass out from pure pleasure.

He released my arms but didn't step away from me. Then he laughed. "A good try, Sami, but next shot, hold your aim."

My vision adjusted. "Crap." The arrow stuck out of the ground at least five feet in front of the target and three feet to the left.

"Dinnae be too worried," he said. "Crossbows are noted for their inaccuracy."

"Really?" I asked, turning so I could see him telling me such a blatant lie to make me feel better.

He nodded, never breaking eye contact.

I've read stupid, romantic stuff about a man devouring a woman with his eyes. I've always thought that was dumb. But I think Adan was doing it to me. I had no idea how to react, so I looked back at the bow. "Can I try again?" I asked.

"Aye."

He stood behind me, and the chivalrous process started over.

Twenty shots later, I could finally hold the crossbow at the correct height and shoot the thing all by myself, although Adan always had to step in and help me load.

Shot thirty-one. I hit the target dead center. The minute the bolt left the bow, I knew it was perfect. Adan laughed and circled his hands around my waist from behind. " 'Tis my bonnie lass," he said. Then he quick-kissed me on the neck. "I can feel your pulse racing here," he whispered, touching another spot with his lips.

Whoa! The advantages of shooting a crossbow are incredible.

Nessie's Shy

That's what Adan said on the ride home.

"She's a timid creature. She doesn't want the world to know she exists. She's content living the old ways deep beneath the water."

I smiled. Adan had done that all afternoon, saying

crazy things about Nessie. He spoke about her like she was a family friend.

It made me want to kiss him.

Wait—maybe I wanted to kiss him because he was so hot and had such great hands. My desire to smooch with him had nothing to do with his spiritual connection to the Loch Ness monster.

Orbs

Fiona has gone crazy. The whole light anomalies/orbs thing is making her think like a possessed witch-hunter. Tonight she brought me a hundred pages of documentation on paranormal light anomalies that she'd found on the Internet.

I have to admit, she's getting me kind of geeked about it. There's a ghost—an unhappy, tormented one named Sam—in my loft.

Maybe Scotland is rubbing off on me. Ghosts, Nessie, clan wars. It's so medieval nutso.

I bet people would pay big bucks to stay in a haunted cottage.

I brought this up to Fiona, but she said it wouldn't

be fair to use Samuel in that way. Like he's an old family friend or something.

I think Fiona's mad at me because I hung out with Adan this afternoon.

Mom told her. Mom can't keep a secret. Note to self: Don't tell Mom anything.

Anyway, Fiona's been grouchy, saying things like "He's a McClintogg." Fiona is mentally stuck in her stupid clan war, but that's her issue. Even if he is a McClintogg, I, a MacKensie — sort of — had a supergreat day with him.

Fiona nudged my ribs with her elbow. We sat on the end of my bed. She turned the digital video recorder so I could see the screen. "There, did you see it?"

"No."

She sighed. "Stop daydreaming about Adan McClintogg and focus." She made his name sound all nasty and evil.

"He's not bad, Fiona," I said. "He packed a lunch and everything."

She harrumphed. "Pay attention to Samuel."

Fiona needs to get a life.

Day 19

Pimples

Two days and I haven't heard from Adan.

My forehead has two pimples and my chin one. This is terrible.

What if Adan sees me like this?

I could always wear a paper sack over my head, not that it matters. I haven't seen Adan. Fiona says it's because McClintoggs only think of themselves, and that to Adan I'm the equivalent of a medieval peasant, while he sees himself as some kind of king.

Fiona needs to learn friend-comforting skills.

Soap

Okay, so we ran out of soap last night, and with my pimple outbreak, that is completely unacceptable.

Mom's catching the MacKensie insanity. She says we'll make our own soap instead of simply finding a store and buying some more.

What is the point of that?

Mom said we should experience everything that future tourists will.

"They can't bring their own soap?" I asked.

"The point of MacKensie Manor running as a working farm is to give people the opportunity to live and participate in all parts of the past," she said. "That means making soap."

"That sounds dumb."

"No," she said. "Dumb is stinking because you don't want to take the time to make soap."

I cracked my pinky knuckle. "What? I don't want to stink. We could just go and buy soap."

"That's not the point. The point is to live the way people did in the past."

"I never asked to live in the past."

She started tapping her right foot, and I knew I was in for it.

"Sami, life isn't always about what you ask for."

I nodded. Mom was in lecture mode, and once she's there, she won't stop.

"We do things sometimes because they're just the right thing to do. And you stink, so we're making soap."

I lifted my right arm and smelled my pit. "I stink?"

Things were going downhill fast. I stank, and the lecture was about to hit me like a speeding train.

"One, Molly and I wrote back and forth for several months before I even learned about her situation, the possibility of their losing their land and all . . . and, two, I offered to help."

"Mom," I said, "I don't care about that. I stink. Can we just go and buy some soap?"

She pulled the large wooden bowl off the shelf, turned, and set it on the table. "Why?" She looked at me, waiting for me to answer.

I sat through ten seconds of silence before I spoke. "Because I'm getting pimples, and I stink."

She shook her head. "Because helping family is the right thing to do. Geez, Sami, I can't believe I've raised someone so selfish. What if we needed their help?"

"Selfish? I'm out there milking, counting sheep,

and cleaning." I pointed at her. "You're using power tools and building things. Doing cool stuff. I"—I pointed at my chest—"am spending every day working with Fiona. She's always talking about ghosts and complaining about the one date I had with Adan while I'm swiping at cobwebs and scrubbing windows. Do you know how hard it is to get all the soap streaks off the glass?"

She shook her head. "It's not about what chores we're doing. It's about helping."

"Fine, then, let's switch partners. I want to use the power tools," I said.

She nodded. "I think that would be great. I'll work with Fiona tomorrow and get to know her. You can work with Molly. Now, go out to our garden and pick some lavender."

I rolled my eyes. "Why?"

She sighed. "Because I need some scent for the soap."

"I don't like lavender."

"Since when?"

I shrugged.

She looked at me like I'd lost my mind. "Fresh lavender in soap is the best."

"How do you know that? It's not like we've ever made soap."

"I have."

I turned to the door. "You mean one of your characters has made it?"

"No, I made it once."

"Why?"

"So the character in my story would know what to do. Writers research, Sami, and then, if possible, live the experience to make it real in the story."

I left, slamming the door. I wish I had a crossbow. I'd go do some target practice or something. I wonder if Fiona has a set of golf clubs. I could swing one of those for a while. I like to do that when I'm frustrated.

Characters in Books Are Not Real People Doing Real Things

Seems logical.

Characters are just that—pretend people with pretend problems. Who cares if they know how to make soap scented with lavender or roses?

I yanked a spear of lavender and pulled the entire plant up. I shook the dirt from the root.

Great.

Mom enjoys doing research. I've always thought it's annoying that she spends so much time getting to know her characters. But learning to make soap just so her character could is . . . cool.

Rats.

But why did she have to pull me into it? I'm not writing a novel. I don't need some killer scene full of details on the art of soapmaking.

I pulled another plant, this time pinching the stem below the blossoms and not yanking out the entire thing. Success!

As much as I hate to admit it, having a mother who writes is pretty cool. I mean, I wouldn't be here in Scotland if she had some other job.

Yeah, maybe someday our family would have traveled to Scotland, but then it would be just as tourists. Seeing a new country as an active part of a family is awesome.

I sighed and yanked out another plant. Shoot.

I hate being wrong, and now I felt bad about saying I didn't get along with Fiona. She's kind of cool.

I hate it when my mouth spits out things I don't really mean.

Now I'll have to apologize. Crap.

Bathing Scars

Okay, I have to admit, the soap does smell good, and it works—I'm clean and I no longer stink. Mom and I boiled extra water, stoked the fire, and filled our bath "tub" to the rim. I've learned to relax in the small tub lined with towels.

There was one slight problem. Mom doesn't know how to extract the fragrance without putting the entire plant in the mixture, stem and all.

We have scratches all over our bodies from the ground lavender stems. It took me about an hour of brushing to get the bits and pieces from my hair, not to mention the fact that it makes terrible conditioner. I freaked out when I saw the pile of hair I'd pulled out just with one swipe of the comb.

Mom said we'll have to keep trying until we get it right. It wouldn't be good for a paying guest to look all beat up after a bath. Mom and I are the guinea pigs.

Yeah, the live-like-a-peasant crash-test dummies.

Mom's Driving Me Nuts

Why do parents (especially my mom) have to know everything? Mom's been grilling me for an hour about my friendship with Fiona and what I think of Adan.

It all started when I asked her to help me comb the knots out of my hair. I sat at the kitchen table while she worked from one knot to another. She had me where she wanted me—helpless and tied up in knots.

She tried keeping her interrogation innocent, but she knew what she was doing. Each strand of hair ripping out from the roots was a message to me: talk or go bald.

"You and Fiona seem to be getting along," she said.

"Yeah. She doesn't shop, though," I said. "And she doesn't like Adan because he's a McClintogg. Oh, and she wants me to help her find Samuel's murderer."

"Samuel?"

"Yes, remember the ghost?"

"Oh yeah."

I nodded. "His name is Samuel Logan, and Fiona is convinced a McClintogg killed him."

"What?"

"Ouch! Come on, Mom, be careful."

"Sorry," she said. "Is that why this Samuel ghost is still around?"

I shrugged. "That's what Fiona thinks."

"Interesting."

Yeah . . . right. That's going into one of her stories.

"Uh-huh," I grunted.

"What about Adan? He seems like a nice boy."

I shrugged. "I haven't heard from him."

"I thought you said the date went well."

I shrugged again. "Yeah."

"Boys can be idiots," said Mom.

"Yeah."

Day 20

Clan Wars

Ten sheep are missing.

Fiona believes the McClintoggs have stolen them.

Whatever. That's the dumbest thing I've ever heard.

Found Sheep

The lost sheep were at some secluded pond taking a break, sleeping in the shade.

Duh, Fiona.

5 p.m.

Mom has been gone all day working with Molly. She said something about using a saw.

I thought I was going to get to work with the power tools.

Guess not.

11 p.m.

Fiona's here. I haven't said anything about the missing sheep and neither has she. It's like it never happened. Weird.

Clan wars, in Fiona's mind, obviously include a healthy dose of denial.

Fiona came armed with her ghost-hunting equipment: a digital camera, digital voice recorder, and one black outfit for each of us. Why? Maybe Samuel will be able to communicate better with us if I'm not wearing tan. Ha.

It's not like we're burglars breaking into someone's house to steal the family diamonds under the cover of darkness.

Who cares if the spirits of the dead see us coming? Maybe light colors would be for the best. Then if the spirits saw us, they'd stay in their spirit world and stop whispering things like "McClintogg."

I looked over Fiona's shoulder at the display screen as she flipped through a recap of the evidence we'd already captured. Even now I saw nothing except a couple of spots of light.

"Tonight's our lucky night," said Fiona. "I can feel it." She turned and looked at me. "We're going to get something."

Samuel Logan ... MacKensie?

Fiona and I sat on my bed. I'd had to change into the black clothes she'd brought me because we were going to sneak onto McClintogg land or something.

"Remember we found birth records of a Samuel Logan MacKensie?" she said. "There wasn't anything about when or how he died. It's like he disappeared."

"Maybe you have the wrong Samuel Logan," I said.

"Impossible. There's only one," she said.

"Seriously? In all of Scotland, there's only one Samuel Logan?"

She sighed and cracked her pinky knuckle—yeah, she does that too. "We're not looking in all of Scotland, Sami. There's only one mentioned in the records of this area."

"Oh."

She pointed to a stack of papers. "Samuel was born in 1272."

"What? Are you serious?" I asked. "I thought he killed himself in the seventeen hundreds, Fiona."

She squinted. "Rumors." She cracked her pinky again. " 'Tis an old country, Sami. 'Twas the time of Sir William Wallace."

It annoys me when Fiona gets all haughty about her country. I don't know why.

She tipped her head toward the stack of papers.

Crap, I couldn't keep quiet. "You're telling me our ghost, Samuel, fought with William Wallace?"

"Wouldn't be so unheard of," Fiona said. "Many men in our village died fighting for their idea of freedom, including some MacKensies."

"Of course," I said, waiting for Fiona to make

some rude comment about the McClintoggs. She can't say something positive about the MacKensies without countering it with something negative about the McClintoggs.

She continued, "McClintoggs fought alongside MacKensies then. We always stand with our countrymen in times of war. McClintogg and MacKensie hatred has nothing to do with the outside world."

I thought for a minute. "So . . . that means neither a McClintogg nor a MacKensie had anything to do with ghost Samuel's death."

Fiona said, "Samuel came back from the war and lived the quiet life of a farmer. That's what the legends say."

"Legends," I said. "It's a bunch of old guys sitting around in a tavern talking."

"Nay," she said. "Don't underestimate hearsay."

I sighed and played along. "So, an uneventful life. That doesn't lead to murder, Fiona. Maybe you're reading too much into what you think you heard on the recording."

She shook her head. "No, I heard the name 'McClintogg,' and so did you, Sami. Something happened."

"There are no records of him either way, living or dead," I said.

"And there's the legend of his hanging himself," Fiona added.

I shrugged. "Maybe it's just that, a legend."

She shook her head. "I dinnae think so. If it was nothing more than a story, the ghost of Samuel wouldn't still be here, speaking to us."

Dressed in Black, Sitting in a Dark Field

Fiona's brilliant idea for the rest of the night consisted of sitting at the edge of a field and watching for signs of ghosts. Battle ghosts, to be precise.

I was beginning to wonder where Fiona was doing her ghost research. According to her, one of her sources at the local market had given eyewitness accounts of seeing soldier ghosts marching in this field, a medieval battlefield. I didn't know what this had to do with Samuel or why others could see ghosts and I couldn't.

"They wear clothing from the Middle Ages," Fiona whispered. "Sometimes they walk around like they're in a camp; other times they charge an unseen enemy, and other times they are bandaged, decapitated, or bloody and stumbling."

Great, she's a ghost-hunting nutso. Her obsessive personality is way out of control.

"What does this have to do with Samuel Logan?" I asked.

She whispered, "If he was a soldier, it'd make sense that he'd show himself on this battlefield. Maybe we'll see him."

"I'm freezing, Fiona."

"Aye," she whispered. "It's the change in temperature that comes before the spirits."

I pulled my knees up and rested my chin on them. This was stupid. "How are we going to know if we see Samuel?"

She pointed. "I've spread special herbs on the ground in front of us. He'll know we're looking for him and come to us."

"What?"

"Aye, he'll come to us."

Must be Samuel didn't want to talk to us, because we sat there from midnight until dawn and nothing, not even one decapitated figure.

Day 21

Double Date

Adan stopped by my cottage this morning. Luckily I took a shower last night in Fiona's bathroom and didn't have any lavender sticks in my hair.

He brought his friend Shane. They wanted to go on a double date, if we could get Fiona to agree. Shane said something about admiring her from afar but not having the courage to speak to her. Their plan involved using me to play matchmaker. Awesome!

Personally, I thought Shane would have better luck asking Fiona out without Adan around, but I guess he was looking for strength in numbers, so the three of us went to MacKensie Castle to find Fiona.

When Fiona saw us, her eyes spit fire at Adan, but she didn't know how to react to Shane. Her split personalities had to be going nuts inside.

At first, I thought she'd grab an ax and chase Adan

off her property, but once Shane climbed out of the car, she turned all shy and quiet.

I swear, she needs some serious counseling.

Hmmmm . . . Fiona likes Shane. That makes my setting them up so much easier.

Not surprisingly, it didn't take too much convincing to get her to agree to go on the double date. She had two rules: one, Adan couldn't speak to her, and two, we had to go and sit in the ghost field.

I don't know how Fiona thought she was going to get a guy with that plan, but Shane seemed thrilled, so she must've known what she was doing. Either that or Shane is as nuts as she is.

We had to convince our moms to let us stay out late again. It wasn't that big a problem, since Mom and Molly think it's cool we're hunting ghosts. Of course, we didn't tell them the guys were going to be with us.

Holding back information isn't lying . . . is it?

Ghost Field Double Date

Since we hadn't told our moms that the guys were going, Fiona and I took off on the four-wheeler at dusk. Adan and Shane were going to meet us there.

Fiona packed way too much stuff. I had to juggle two backpacks and two sleeping bags on my lap while she whipped across the field. I almost fell off the back three times.

I know she was trying to dump me. She wasn't happy about spending the night in a field with Adan McClintogg. She'd mumbled about the "stinking McClintoggs" while she'd packed.

She must really like Shane.

When we got to the rendezvous location, the guys were already there. They'd dug a shallow pit, circled it with stones, and had a nice fire going. It got cold at night here. Fiona wouldn't have a fire the other night—something about frightening the spirits away.

The guys' sleeping bags were rolled out, and there was a pile of food sitting on one. From the looks of it, they planned on eating all night. Guys eat like horses, I swear. I wouldn't be eating a thing.

Speaking of horses, apparently they'd ridden out to the meeting spot, because two horses stood in the shadows, tied to a large stake.

Fiona didn't like the fire. She said, "What are ye thinking? We won't see any ghosts with that going."

Shane said, "Aye, we will, Fiona," and winked at her.

Fiona got this soft, mushy look in her eyes, and nodded like she was starring in one of Mom's romance novels. The big, strong hero says it's fine, and the heroine just goes along with it. Disgusting!

If they acted like this all night, I'd scream.

I put the backpacks by the fire and spread out our sleeping bags a suitable distance from the guys'.

"What's the plan, Fiona?" Adan asked, breaking rule number one—no talking between the two of them.

Fiona glared at him. "Dinnae be talking to me, Adan McClintogg."

"Fiona, it'll be a long night if there's no talking," Shane said.

"We can talk. Just Adan and I won't," she said.

She sat on her sleeping bag and Shane plopped down on mine beside her. "He's not so bad, Fiona."

"Aye, he is, Shane. And if ye've come to make peace between the McClintoggs and MacKensies, ye're wasting your time."

Shane shook his head. "This is foolish, Fiona. MacKensies and McClintoggs haven't feuded in years."

"Aye," said Fiona. "Then my dad died. Ye tell him to leave my family alone."

Shane looked into the fire. "I'll not spend my night speaking between the two of you. Tell him yourself."

"I already have," she said.

"Then you've said your piece."

"Aye."

Adan sat on the bag with all the food and I sat down next to him. "I dinnae want yer family home, Fiona," he said.

We'd never see any ghosts if these two kept up this argument. The night was quickly turning into a therapy session.

"Aye, ye do, Adan McClintogg," Fiona said. "Dinnae lie because yer friend is here."

Adan shook his head. "Not even my father who runs the clan . . . "

Fiona covered her ears.

Adan sighed and quit talking.

11 p.m.

I probably have burned marshmallow stuck between my teeth. I broke my "no eating in front of guys" rule and ate toasted marshmallows.

I couldn't resist.

11:05 p.m.

Adan made a pot of tea. They drink a lot of tea in Scotland.

It was good. Even Fiona complimented him on it.

Progress?

Day 22

Midnight

Under Fiona's protests that we wouldn't see ghosts if there was a fire, the guys compromised. Our once mighty fire became nothing but smoldering coals. I was sitting close, and my front was warm, but my back and butt were freezing.

Fiona and I properly sat on our side of the fire and the guys sat on theirs.

There were no ghosts, but that didn't bother me. I was happy spending time with Adan. The light from the fire made him look so gorgeous.

2:16 a.m.

This sucked. I was the only one awake. I tried to sleep, but it was too cold . . . and too quiet.

3:10 a.m.

Almost fell asleep.

3:12 a.m.

Heard a noise. What was it?
    I started hyperventilating.
    Cats?

3:17 a.m.

The noises of dying cats have been replaced by eerier sounds—moaning, thumps, sobbing.

Holy crap. I didn't want to see a spirit carrying his bloody, decapitated head.

I shook Fiona. "Wake up," I whispered.

She bolted out of her sleeping bag, grabbed her camcorder, and hit Record, sweeping the lens back and forth over the dark field. "What is it?" she asked. "Did ye see something?"

That woke the guys. "What is it?" asked Shane. "Do ye have something on camera?" He moved over and stood by Fiona.

Adan came over and sat by me. "Did ye see something?" he whispered.

"No," I said.

"Heard something, then?"

"Yes."

He didn't ask any more questions. Feeling that I didn't want to talk about it, he just nodded and put his arm around me.

3:25 a.m.

I kept pinching myself to keep from crying. I sat snuggled next to Adan and hadn't heard any moaning for almost nine minutes. During that time Fiona and Shane had left the security of our camp, wandered out onto the field, and come back. They both had genuine looks of disappointment on their faces.

"Nothing," said Fiona.

That was a good thing. Right?

"Fiona," Adan said, "did you get any sounds?"

"No," said Shane. "We already did a playback of the audio. Nothing."

Adan pulled me closer. "Sami heard something," he said.

Fiona and Shane nodded. "Aye," said Shane. "What'd ye hear, Sami? What'd it sound like?"

"Moaning. Cats."

"Ghost moaning?" asked Fiona.

Adan laughed. "We're sitting in the middle of a battlefield, Fiona, waiting for the spirits of the dead. Is there another kind of moaning?"

Fiona smiled. "No."

"Let's go home," said Adan. "I think Sami's had enough."

I hated being the coward. Adan hugged me and told me it was fine.

"Ye can hear the spirits, Sami," said Shane.

"No," I said.

"Aye, ye can, Sami," said Adan. He pulled me into his arms. "You'll be our medium, our connection to the dead."

"What?" I looked around our small circle. They were all nodding.

Fiona clapped her hands. "It'll be perfect. That's why we haven't seen a ghost, Sami," she said. "We need someone to communicate with them and let them know it's safe to show themselves to us . . . to come back into our world."

"What?" I sounded like a recording.

"Aye, do ye think so, Fiona?" asked Shane.

She nodded. "All spirits need something to communicate through. It'll be Sami." She smiled at me.

"We'll use that to our advantage," said Adan.

"What?" I cried again.

They'd all eaten too many marshmallows.

4:30 a.m.—Back at the Cottage

Maybe ghosts do talk to me.

Not cool.

During our time on the battlefield, Adan and Fiona had apparently worked through their family squabbles — at least enough to agree that I was some weird clairvoyant, and that the four of us would try to communicate with the dead again. Or should I say, they were going to use me to communicate with the dead.

I don't want to speak to the dead, and I don't want them talking to me. Why don't they just talk to Fiona and leave me alone?

Wool Dyeing

Molly, Fiona, Mom, and I dyed wool today.

Fiona explained that this was another activity they were trying to perfect for future guests. So I was off to be the test dummy again.

I'm still wondering who would pay for this type of vacation. But if they put ghost tours on the agenda, I think the place would be swamped with paying paranormal weirdos. They'd pay more than those zany want-to-go-back-to-the-past type people. There are always shows on television about people wanting to vacation in haunted hotels and stuff.

I was so tired, and my ideas about chilling and catching up on my sleep did not include dipping wool into boiling vats of colored water. *Oh well, here goes nothing.*

Molly and Mom had things set up by the smallest cottage, the one Fiona and I had cleaned earlier in the week. It's the one I wish Mom and I were staying in. There's a pond in the backyard, no loft, and no Samuel Logan.

The dyeing area consisted of three huge pots, each sitting on its own stack of wood. There were also three long wooden tables and a huge wood-framed box with chicken wire across the bottom.

Mom was carrying a bucket of water and dumped it into the middle pot. Molly walked among the three tables, piling each with weeds.

"Mum's found some recipes for medieval wool dye," Fiona said as we walked closer. "I think she's working on yellow today."

"Yellow?"

"Aye, before you came we worked on brown," Fiona said. "Mum tries different mixtures until she gets the best color. That will be the formula she'll use when the guests dye wool."

I watched Molly separate a bunch of plants. "Is she going to use that?"

"Aye."

Mom called. "Hey, girls, grab some buckets and help me fill the last two cauldrons."

We did. By the time we finished, we had a path of worn grass between the pond and the work station. It took a million buckets to half fill the pots; maybe Molly should hook up some kind of a hose system. I mentioned this to Fiona, and she looked at me like I wanted to spoil all the wool-dyeing fun.

Mom lit the fires, and Molly gave everyone an apron. Mine had brown stains all over it—maybe from Molly's earlier wool-dyeing experiments. Then Molly walked us over to the tables and explained each plant.

"Lady's Bedstraw will give a cheese-yellow color," she said. "Chamomile is supposed to give a strong yellow. And onion peels will give a yellow or orange."

"Did you grow these here?" Mom asked.

"Not yet," said Molly. "First I'll find the color I like the most, and then we'll plant. I want to have enough so we can harvest and dye twice each summer. I'm going to use walnut husks for the brown."

Mom nodded like she knew what Molly was talking about. I didn't have a clue, but it was kind of cool because I felt like a medieval mad scientist, working in my outdoor lab.

"In one of your novels," Fiona said to Mom, "the lady dyed wool. I remember reading it."

Mom smiled. "Yeah, I researched that scene." She looked at the plants on the table. "I'm a little nervous doing this. I hope I wasn't too far off."

"Auch, no, you weren't," said Fiona. "I helped Mom with the brown. Walnut was what was used in your book. It's a good color."

Mom smiled.

"Dyeing wool makes for a long day," said Fiona.

"That's the way I wrote it," said Mom.

Mom and Fiona walked to the cauldrons together to stoke the fires.

Molly looked at me. "Fiona likes reading," she said.

I nodded. Weird.

"Want to help me tear these, Sami?" she asked, standing at the table full of onion peels.

"Yeah."

"Is it hard having a mom who's a writer?"

"No," I lied. It *was* tough. Sometimes Mom would go into her writing mode and not come out of it for days.

"Auch, Sami," Molly sighed. "My mum was a painter. I hated it and told myself I'd never do anything creative if it meant not spending time with my kids. So I know what it's like to live with an artist."

I grabbed an onion out of a large sack and ripped the skin off. "I try not to let it bother me," I said, feeling comfortable talking with Molly.

"Aye." Molly stood beside me removing an onion skin. "It's something to be proud of, but that doesna make it easy."

"Yeah."

"My mum would paint me. She used to sell her work to a little shop in town. They couldn't keep her paintings in the store. Tourists would snap them up," she said.

I looked at her. "So you could be hanging on the wall of some stranger's house?"

She laughed. "Aye. It used to give me nightmares."

"And now?"

She sighed. "Her paintings hang in my bedroom. They're more valuable to me than anything else I own."

"I don't like romance novels," I said.

Molly smiled. "Every girl wants a little romance,"

she said. "Have you ever read one of your mum's stories?"

"Yes. Well, no, not really. I was always kind of embarrassed to say my mom wrote romance novels."

"Why?"

"Sounds weird."

"I understand," she said. "But you should read one, Sami. They're very adventurous."

I wish Mom wrote mysteries.

Molly started talking about her mother again. "She painted portraits of people in traditional Highland clothing. I always wore very modern clothing, just to rebel."

"Yeah," I said.

I'm Allergic to Wool

Luckily, all the wool had been spun. I hadn't even thought about that. It would stink to have to spin it like in "Rumpelstiltskin."

Molly had five monster-sized black bags full of wool. It looked like rope, nothing like yarn, and felt soft, like a kitten. Twenty minutes after I'd stuck my hands into a bag to grab some, I broke out in a rash up past my elbows.

It itched like crazy.

I'm going to go insane . . . and be all scabby.

Four Hours Later

Dyeing wool is an all-day process. We had to let the wool, plants, and water all boil f-o-r-e-v-e-r.

But it was okay because Mom and Molly had spread blankets on the ground and brought food. Fiona and I tried to take naps, but our moms kept grilling us about ghosts and what we'd seen or heard during our vigil on the battlefield.

By the time we started pulling the wool out of the dye concoctions and placing it on the drying racks, which were the huge wooden frames with chicken wire across the bottom so the wool could drip-dry evenly, our moms knew that Fiona hadn't caught any visual or auditory evidence on tape. They also knew she thought I was some weird clairvoyant.

I put on thick rubber gloves that covered my rash and would keep the dye off my skin.

We started with the Lady's Bedstraw. Molly stuck a long wooden paddle into the mixture, dipped it to the bottom, and lifted. A pile of gross-looking yellow wool came out. Fiona, Mom, and I, all wearing rubber gloves, grabbed the pile and heaved it over to the drying rack.

"This is a disgusting color, Mum," Fiona said.

"Aye," Molly said. "We'll see how it dries."

Then we fished the wool from the other two cauldrons and spread it out to dry.

My favorite was the onion-peel-dyed wool. It was a strong yellow with an undertone of orange. I'd buy a sweater that color—just not in wool.

Day 23

Great

I apparently rubbed my hand across my right cheek while pulling out the gross Lady's Bedstraw wool.

There's a disgusting streak of cheese yellow going

from my chin to my temple, and it keeps getting darker. Molly says it will continue to darken until the chemicals from the plants have finished setting. I tried to wash it off with our lavender soap. No luck.

I look like some alien from a bad science fiction movie—the alien with the cheese-cheek and rash clear up to her shoulders.

I'm not leaving the cottage until both are gone. Molly says it could take days.

I bet this never happened in one of Mom's romances.

Day 24

Creature from the Dye Pit

I'm so freaky-looking that even Samuel won't come and talk to me.

The cottage is quiet, and Mom made me stay home with this stinky poultice wrap on my hands and arms. I'm a cheese-faced mummy.

Date with a Stained Face

Shane called Fiona and said that he and Adan wanted to take us on a ghost tour. It would be an overnight stay in the underground city, which consists of hidden tunnels beneath the village.

"Have you ever been?" I asked Fiona.

"No, we locals don't go to the tourist places," she said.

I understood that. I'd never been to the antique malls in Abbey, Michigan, but people came from all over to spend the day looking at what I thought was other people's old junk.

"When do they want to go?" I asked.

"Tonight."

"Fiona, I still have cheese-cheek." It'd been two days, and the stain had lightened some. But to see Adan with my discolored face? Not to mention the leftover scabs on my arms from my allergic reaction to the wool.

Fiona laughed. "They'll understand."

"Who understands something like this?" I touched my cheek.

"They already called the tour company and booked

the tour for the four of us." She wouldn't make eye contact.

"Fiona," I sighed.

She shrugged. "I already told them yes."

"Fiona," I growled. "So, I can't say no."

"I dinnae think ye'll want to miss it," she said. "The underground ghost tour is supposed to be the best in all Scotland. Well, not including the one in Edinburgh."

I knew it'd be fun. But . . . "My cheek," I said.

Fiona smiled. "I have an idea to cover it, but I dinnae think Adan will mind. He's always liked history, and yer face is part of a historical scientific experiment."

"Ha, funny." I moaned. "What's your idea? Makeup won't cover it. I already tried."

"A scarf," she said, sounding confident.

"Scarf? I'm not wearing a scarf around my head."

"Then just tell the truth," she said.

Yeah, Adan, hope you like yellow. At least I can cover my arms with a long-sleeved shirt.

"We'll have fun," Fiona said.

"What's it like?" I tried to forget about my face.

She shrugged. "From what I've heard, a guide walks us through the tunnels under the town telling us scary stories."

"Interesting."

"Aye, most villages, towns, and cities in Scotland have underground vaults and tunnels."

"I'm not communicating with spirits, Fiona. When we're in the tunnels, don't mention anything about me talking to ghosts," I said.

She smiled.

"Wouldn't dream of it," she said. "But ye can, Sami."

Underground-Tunnel Ghost Tour

Molly was thrilled we were going on the tour; a "perilous crusade," she called it. She said she'd gone once with Fiona's dad when they first started dating and had never forgotten it, maybe because it was the first time he'd kissed her.

Mom said that was romantic. Fiona blushed, and I knew she was thinking of Shane because she was cracking her right pinky. She has the hots for him. Majorly.

I didn't think it was romantic or adventurous. I was worried. I cracked my left pinky finger so many times that afternoon, I'm lucky it didn't fall off.

What if ghosts really did want to talk to me? Samuel Logan freaked me out enough. Imagine an entire underground city full of Samuels all clamoring to communicate with me. That'd suck.

Holy crap.

By the time we met the guys in town, I was a worked-up, anxious nutcase. The stain on my cheek was pushed so far back in my terror-stricken mind that I'd actually forgotten it was there until Adan saw it, leaned in to kiss me, and said, "Fiona told me about the wool-dyeing. 'Tis beautiful."

The compliment helped me relax, but my complexion wasn't at the top of my things-to-worry-about-right-now list. Adan grabbed my hand, and my heart raced even faster.

I'd walk with him into a pit full of Scottish spirits.

He stood next to me. "I won't leave your side, Sami," he said.

I nodded. Why was I such a baby? I felt stupid but couldn't stop my fear. Something wasn't right about this tunnel. Something in my gut was shouting, Don't go in there, Sami.

Adan gently moved me forward. I breathed deeply and swallowed. The tour guide, a man in his fifties dressed as a medieval Scottish warrior, complete with claymore, met us at a big wooden door. His voice was deep and slow. "Gaun-to-doo," he said, turning to push open the door.

I looked at Fiona. "Death's door," she translated.

Figures. The guide walked ahead of us, holding a dim lantern above his head. Fiona and Shane went first. I followed Shane, and Adan brought up the rear.

Small fire sconces lit our way through the dark. Despite the width of the passage, I felt the walls closing in around me. The place smelled like burning candles and moss.

The guide was talking but I couldn't focus on his words. His eyes would look wild when he'd stop, turn, point to something, and tell us about some tragic or violent death. When he talked about the spirits that wandered the tunnels, his eyes would get wide and dart back and forth, back and forth.

Adan leaned forward and whispered in my ear, "He's good."

I nodded. I was trying not to process the guide's words. I knew if I did, I'd run for it.

At a crucial point in a story, the guide made a small lunge toward Fiona. She jumped and then started laughing. Shane joined her.

What was wrong with them? Didn't they know we were at death's door, for crying out loud? That was no laughing matter.

The tour continued: on and on, around a corner to the right, then back to the left; into a large cavern, through a tight passage, right, left.

Luckily, I'd worn my hiking boots. We must have walked about five miles. The underground city was larger than the entire village of Beauly. The guide stopped in a large cavern, where we sat on rocks that had been set up to look like bleachers.

He told us we'd been in the tunnels for two hours, and that it was now time for him to leave. He'd return at two a.m. to finish the tour.

"What?" I asked. "You're leaving us here? Fiona?"

She shrugged and cracked her right pinky.

I snapped my left one.

"We have a map," Adan said. He opened his pack and took out two water bottles. "Water and snacks," he said as he continued to pull things out. "Two flashlights. If ye get too frightened, we can find an exit."

I looked around. The guide had disappeared with his lantern. Our guiding light. I hoped Adan had new batteries in his flashlights.

"Let's go sit in the first chamber," Shane said.

"Aye," Adan and Fiona said at the same time.

"This isn't a tour . . . it's a tomb," I mumbled.

Can You Die from Fear?

I thought I was going to have a heart attack. My headstone would say something like "She died on a ghost tour. Sorry, no refunds."

Poltergeist or Shadow?

From my extensive experience watching shows about ghosts and reading Fiona's research, I know that poltergeist activity involves objects being thrown or otherwise moved.

I heard a small pebble bounce across the stone floor, and it hit my boot. Adan said he'd accidentally kicked it, but I couldn't see his face, so I figured he'd said that so I wouldn't pee my pants.

Fiona said she saw something move across the path in front of her and Shane, but Shane insisted it was just the shadow cast from his flashlight.

I'm breaking out in a cold sweat. I have goose bumps. I'm going to croak.

Small Chamber

The small chamber had been at the beginning of the tour. We backtracked, following Shane's guiding light. The guide and map both said the ghost of a grouchy old man haunts this tiny room.

"The guide said he pushes people," Adan said. He punched Shane in the arm.

"And steals women's jewelry." Shane laughed.

The four of us sat waiting in that creepy room for at least an hour, but nothing happened. Thank goodness. I took deep breaths. At least the air was cooler in here.

We studied the map of the tunnels and read the explanations of spirit activity and where it occurred. After a while the quietness of the room, the comforting closeness of the others—two of them hot, strong guys—relaxed me.

By the time we had a new plan of attack, I had found my inner fount of ghost-hunting courage.

What did I have to be frightened of, anyway? Even if there were ghosts, they couldn't hurt me. Ghosts are just flimsy mists. Right?

The Hunt

We decided to continue our exploring in the northern tunnels. The guys, rather heroically, let us walk in front of them. I was fine with their machismo, since I didn't want to push the limits of my newfound confidence.

In his backpack, Adan had snuck in the cameras and video recorders. Fiona and I armed ourselves with the digital cameras, while the guys took the voice recorders.

Our goal was to collect evidence of paranormal activity.

"Maybe we'll get our own TV show," I said, trying to keep my tone light. "You know, we'd be a new angle: teen ghost hunters."

"Why would we do that?" Fiona asked.

"It'd be cool."

Fiona laughed. "Sami, you are so funny."

"I was being serious."

"Fine, but I dinnae think you'd make a good ghost hunter."

I wasn't offended; she was right. "But I don't have to be good. I'd be the one who's always all freaked out and stuff. It'd be great."

I was so wrapped up in the conversation with Fiona that I kind of forgot the guys were behind us. I heard the gravel crunch and felt a tiny vibration of movement coming from the ground and straight through my right heel.

Ghost. "Crap, crap, crap!" I pushed Fiona to the side and ran past her. I had no clue where I was headed. I just ran.

"Sami!" Fiona yelled.

"Not stopping!" I shouted back over my shoulder.

She followed me. For all the farm work she did, Fiona didn't have much stamina. I, on the other hand, with a ghost chasing me, could go for miles at a sprint.

Lights flashed behind me, making me feel like I was in a stone disco. I don't know how, but Fiona was taking pictures while she ran.

I slowed. Wait . . . was the ghost in front of us? "Crap. Crap." Gravel slid under my feet, I'd braked so fast.

Fiona plowed into my back. "Sami, for the love of all that is good," she said.

She jerked again as Adan ran into her, and then one more time when Shane hit them. "What are ye doing?" asked Adan.

"What am I doing?" I said, feeling stupid. "There was a ghost back there."

"Really?" Shane asked. "Cool."

Adan moved to stand beside me. "Are ye sure, Sami?"

"Yes." Well, technically I wasn't. I was losing my mind. The tunnels were getting to me.

"Did you get any pictures, Fiona?" Shane asked.

I bent over, resting my hands on my knees. "Of what?" I asked.

Fiona laughed. "I dinnae. I just turned, snapped a few shots, and tried to catch something on film."

I straightened. "Do you have anything?"

"Nope," Shane said, looking at the LCD monitor over Fiona's shoulder.

"Not even a wee bit of a thing?" I asked, trying my Scottish accent.

Fiona laughed so hard she snorted. If she'd had a drink of milk, it would have come out her nose. "Ye'd"—she gulped—"make a fine host of a ghost hunt."

Adan and Shane both laughed. "Wee bit," Adan said, hugging me. "You're a funny lass, Sami."

Hate Ghost Hunting

Nothing's happening. Not that I really want anything to happen ghost-wise, but a picture or recorded sound would be cool.

We heard what we thought were ghosts a couple of times, but nothing would record. It sounded like laughing coming from the other side of the tunnel system.

Ghost-Whisperer

Adan and I sat on a rock outside the tunnel exit. Between the stuffy air and the stress of listening for ghosts, I had a splitting headache. Adan had volunteered to sit with me while Shane and Fiona did one final sweep of the tunnels with the cameras and recorders.

Adan put his right arm around my shoulder and began to gently rub the base of my neck. I relaxed as he worked out the tension. My head lolled forward so my chin rested on my chest. My body went limp.

Not one ghost had talked to me the entire time. I was fine with my lack of spiritual communication skills. "The dead don't talk to me," I said.

"Aye," Adan said. "Not tonight."

About half an hour later, Fiona and Shane walked out of the tunnels, followed by the guide. Fiona sat beside me. "Nothing," she said.

"Not so much as a groan," Shane said.

"No light anomalies . . . nothing." Fiona lifted her arms and let her hands flop onto her knees in a sign of surrender.

"I don't understand," said Adan. "Spirits walk the tunnels. Everyone knows it."

"Aye," Shane and Fiona said.

Adan stood up. "A waste of time," he said, shrugging.

Shane stretched out his hand to help Fiona up. "Not entirely," he said, pulling her to her feet and kissing her on the cheek.

I heard Fiona sigh, a true sign that she was head over heels for Shane. Awesome.

Adan took my left hand. The streetlights created an eerie fluorescent glow. Our footsteps echoed in the silence of the early morning, bouncing back and forth between the stone walls of the buildings. A light fog covered the ground.

A small alley veered off the village's one street and to the right. I heard the clip-clopping sounds of horses' hooves on stone. I'd never heard horses' hooves on stone, but I registered the sound the way I'd recognize the sound of water dripping from a faucet. Instinct made me turn to the right, toward the dark alley, toward the sound.

Every nerve, every cell in my body froze. My stopping brought Adan to a standstill. "What?" he whispered. "What do you see, Sami?"

I forced myself to take a breath. "Don't you see it?"

Fiona and Shane stopped and stood next to us. "What is it?" said Fiona.

I shook my head. My brain saw the ghost, but forming words was not possible. I knew I was looking at a ghost. He sat on a Highland pony like Adan's. His white shirt was torn and hung at his waist, and blood trickled from the base of his neck in a stream down his chest. His left arm was raised, and in his hand he held a monster sword. He nodded.

My eyes locked with his. I felt the war inside me. The logical part of my brain knew I should be running, but I couldn't help staring. The spirit glowed. I smiled.

I blinked, and he was gone.

"I think I got a picture," Shane said.

Day 25

Chores

Bessie the cow and I are getting along better. We have our tag-team milking system down. While I'm milking, I talk to her like she's a friend. I tell jokes, and she moo-laughs and stands still.

This morning I talked to her about how everyone keeps saying I can see ghosts and how they claim to have photographic evidence. Bessie is on my side; she mooed, confirming that they didn't. The one picture Shane snapped looked like nothing more than a double exposure.

After a few hours of sleep, I've convinced myself that the ghost on the horse was probably a product of my overtired imagination.

The cheese stain on my cheek is gone!

And I'm not imagining that!

Fair

The annual fair will be in the village on Saturday. Mom, Molly, Fiona, and I are going. Molly has rented a booth, where she's going to begin her advertising venture for her living medieval farm.

I'm still not sure who she thinks will visit the manor. Fiona is as delusional as her mom about it. Even my mom has bought into it.

They're all nuts. But since the fair is full of people from the Society for Creative Anachronism, all those nutso people will fit in.

Day 28

Medieval Fair

It's quite a show of peasant proportions.

Help! I'm stuck in a world of people who think it's cool to live in cold castles, wear hundreds of pounds of armor, and have no electricity or flushing toilets.

Wool Stockings

Not only do I have to go to this fair, I have to dress like a medieval commoner.

What will Adan think?

He'll be dressed in his I'm-a-Scottish-knight-on-holiday outfit, and I'll be walking around wearing a dress that looks like a potato sack.

Apparently, Molly sewed the outfits herself. I look

like a fat cow in it. I could be Bessie's sister. I told Mom that, and she told me to grow up.

How can I grow up if I have to go out in public dressed like I just walked out of some low-budget Halloween costume store?

This will be the worst-dressed moment of my life.

I didn't think it could be any worse than the cheese stain, but I was wrong.

At least I'm not wearing the tall wool socks. Mom said she didn't want to hear me whine about the rash I'd get from the wool, so now I have to wear my tennis shoes.

I'm going to look so dumb.

At least Mom, Molly, and Fiona all have similar potato-sack dresses. I'll fit in with the losers.

Knights and Ladies

Everyone was dressed in costume. I've got to admit that being in the village dressed like all the weirdos was kind of fun. Although it took me a while to get past my jealousy—some girls had on awesome dresses. I'd have given my blow-dryer to wear some of them.

Mom said, "Everyone likes to play dress-up, but most of the people here would never even have seen material that expensive if they'd really lived during medieval times."

Molly laughed. "We all can't be the queen."

It took us an hour to set up the booth. We'd just hung the last clump of dried lavender when the first person arrived. By lunchtime, Molly had two pages of e-mail and snail-mail addresses from people requesting information. They weren't just being polite, either.

For lunch, Fiona and I ate potato soup out of a bread bowl and sat listening to the catchy tunes people sang as they strolled past our booth. My foot tapped to the sounds, and by early afternoon I was whistling some pub tune about a lady and her secret boyfriend. The out-of-place feeling I'd started the morning with was completely gone.

Even with my white tennis shoes sticking out of the bottom of my peasant dress, I was born for medieval fairs.

Flowers

Adan brought me a bouquet of flowers that he'd picked up at one of the booths because he said they'd made him think of me.

He's smooth, and I bought it. In my lifetime, how many Scottish nobles dressed in traditional Highland clothing will give me flowers?

I'm pretty sure the answer is only one — Adan.

Molly braided the smaller buds into my hair.

Scots Are Sooo Hot

Although I'm still not crazy about history and romance novels, I now understand why Mom sets so many of her stories in medieval Scotland. The guys here — Adan mostly, in his medieval noble clothing — are so hot. Like steaming hot, as in I'd let them sweep me off my size nine peasant feet and drag me to their castle to make out with me.

Adan's wearing a kilt, and his knees look delicious. His wool knee socks are straight and perfect. How does he do that? Mine would be bunched around my ankles.

The men are all buff and brooding like they've just lost their best friend, and it's become my task to make them smile.

Mom told Adan I was a hopeless flirt. He just laughed and said, "As long as I get most of it."

Two things were weird about that conversation. For one, Mom doesn't usually like the guys I date. She says they're all losers. But she's okay with Adan. When Molly and I were at the booth alone, she told me that Mom thought Adan was good for me. I asked her why, and she just shrugged and said, "She sees the spark in your eye."

Great. So now I'm one of Mom's hopelessly romantic, sparkling-eyed heroines.

Molly said she liked the way Adan and I were helping Fiona deal with her "misplaced anger."

The second weird thing was, Adan was really mellow about my flirting. American guys get all bent out of shape if their girl even looks at another guy. But Adan just watched me and smiled. He said it was a compliment to him that other guys thought I was attractive; it made him feel good about the attention I gave him. "Women flirt," he said, shrugging. "But I know you'll be dancing with me later. That's what matters." Then he hugged me . . . right in front of Mom.

Ghost Sam

I swear I saw my ghost Samuel standing at the corner eating a turkey leg.

I turned away.

Love

I totally love the smell and taste of fresh bread. It tops my love for spending an entire day at the mall.

Molly's booth is set up in front of a little baker's shop. The lady who runs it has to be about the same age as my grandma Ames, and like Grandma, Christina Muir is petite.

I'd be big as a barn if I worked in her shop. I'd eat the bread all day, end up with an addiction, and have to attend some type of dough lovers' therapy group.

About once an hour Christina brings us warm, fresh-from-the-oven bread. It's no use fighting the aroma or temptation, so I just eat it.

Spending Money

Fiona and Molly brought two large baskets of dried lavender, homemade beeswax candles, and skeins of dyed wool for trading at the market square.

With Adan and Shane off for a couple of hours playing with swords, big stones, and other weapons, we would have time to do some damage before meeting them later at the dance.

"I'm taking Sami," Molly said. "Now I'll show ye a taste of real shopping." She winked at me, then looked at Fiona.

Fiona turned to my mom. "And we'll be coming home with more. I'm a wiser shopper than Mum."

Molly laughed. "A contest ye'll be losing, Fiona."

"Auch, Mum," Fiona said. "The first booth ye see with baubles, ye'll stop and trade all your lavender."

"Aye, I do like the shinny things." Molly took my arm. "Let's go, Sami."

As we walked away Fiona said, "What about the booth?"

"Christina has closed," Molly said. "The smell of her bread brought people down this way. We mid as well close too."

"Aye," Fiona said. "We'll meet back here in an hour?"

"Two," Molly said. "Sami and I have some serious shopping to do."

Molly is So Cool

I wish my mom was as cool as Molly. I thought I was a serious shopper, but Molly made me look like an amateur. I guess it's easy to shop with a credit card or a pocketful of cash, but try going to a shopping mall with a basket of lavender, candles, and soap and see how much you get. Not a pair of American Eagle jeans, that's for sure.

There were two aisles of booths, intersecting at the large market square. Each vendor on one of the main aisles had a booth made of a three-sided tent or tightly woven sticks. The open side faced the shopper.

Molly shopped the way I did. We walked the market and examined all the goods before making any purchases. People were selling the coolest stuff. One lady was selling stained glass she had made herself. An old guy had ancient-looking wooden crates in which perched live hooded falcons. He was selling falcons . . . at the medieval mall.

As we walked, people shouted out, barking their goods, trying to get passersby to stop. I'd just gotten to the point where I could understand Molly, Adan, Fiona, and Shane. But I was lost here. Molly said a lot of the vendors were speaking Gaelic.

I saw a girl my age in jeans and a T-shirt, exactly what I'd be wearing if Molly hadn't made us all our medieval peasant outfits. I felt proud. Even with tennis shoes that didn't fit the peasant theme, I looked like I belonged. I was living the history of the village and wasn't just an ordinary tourist.

Small groups of people stood around gossiping and laughing. A cell phone rang; mine had been dead since I'd gotten off the plane. But I didn't miss it. There's more to life than texting.

Holy cow. I was losing my mind . . . and loving it.

My Future

Molly and I walked near a purple and orange tent. "I've always liked lists and goals," she said.

"The facts," I said.

"Aye."

Unlike at the other booths, this tent's front flap was down, but a round sign scrolled out the word "Fortune" in fancy gold letters.

Once, on the Internet, I'd clicked this fortune-telling site for a free trial. I'd had to answer a bunch of questions, and all I'd gotten in return was some lame form-letter response with my name plugged into key spots. I'd had no interest in the art of prediction since.

"It's good to experience different kinds of things in life," Molly said. "Dinnae ye think?"

She had a point. "Yeah."

"Shall we put our lists and facts away for an hour, Sami, and try a different approach?"

I nodded. "Sure, why not?"

We walked toward the tent arm in arm. We moved slowly, as if we were headed into the principal's office. The flap flew open. A middle-aged man walked out—

well, more like ran. His forehead was wrinkled with concern, or was it fear?

We looked at each other, took a breath, and walked in.

"Velkom." The voice sounded like it belonged to a female Dracula. A woman stepped out from a dark corner. Her blue dress shimmered as she moved slowly, dragging the hem on the wool rug. "My name is Lucia."

She looked like a Gypsy woman I'd seen in an old black-and-white movie. She wore a gold turban on her head. A fake red gem was pinned in the center, holding the turban together. Black curls escaped from the sides and framed her face. Her dark eyes were painted with rich purple shadow. I envied her eye-liner; I never could put it on that straight. I wondered if it was tattooed.

I felt Molly's hand tighten on my forearm and heard the cough of laughter she tried to hide.

Lucia walked over to us, placing one hand on each of our shoulders. "Oh." She pulled back like we'd shocked her. "You are kindred souls."

Molly coughed again. I bit my bottom lip.

"You've come to have your futures told?" she said.

She'd hit the nail on the head. I bit my lip harder. Molly hiccupped and nodded.

"You've come just in time," she said.

"Have we, now?" Molly asked. She wiped the back of her hand across her right eye.

Was she crying? Like laughing crying? I snapped my left pinky finger to control my own laughter.

Lucia looked at Molly's basket. "You've goods to trade?"

"Aye." Molly held out the basket to her.

"It's less than my usual fee," Lucia said. "I'll take the entire basket."

What did she usually charge . . . two live chickens and five bundles of lavender?

"We'd trade it all for a reading," said Molly.

Lucia looked deep into my eyes. I nodded my agreement. There was nothing else at the fair we wanted to buy. Besides, there were tons of lavender and dyed wool back at the cottage. Anyone would've done the same. When you're in a dark tent faced with a lady wearing a golden towel with a fake ruby on it, you'll pay to hear what she has to say.

"Done." Lucia pulled the flap of the tent into place. A few oil lamps cast an eerie, pale light throughout the interior.

"Fortune-tellers work better in the dark," Molly whispered.

I looked at Lucia to make sure she hadn't heard.

Molly leaned in close, whispering, "Do ye think she has a crystal ball?"

Geez. I looked behind us to where Lucia was tying the flap shut. I bet Molly got in trouble all the time in school for talking in class, just like I do.

We sat. My right leg bounced against Molly's left. I was so jumpy. Mom would be putting her hand firmly on my thigh right about now, but Molly's leg bounced faster than mine.

Lucia sat across from us. She reached down, brought up a huge crystal ball, and placed it in the center of the table.

Molly coughed again, hiding her laughter. I bit my lip. My stomach hurt. I was going to crack any second, and not just my left pinky.

I smelled the fog machine working before the clouds started to creep up from under the table.

My bottom lip was numb from biting so hard. My stomach was cramping from trying not to laugh.

Lucia waved her hands dramatically over the ball and closed her eyes. "Come and speak to me, spirits of those who've passed before us. Show me these ladies' futures."

Molly looked at me and winked. Along with my numb lip and cramped stomach, my cheeks were losing sensation because I couldn't stop smiling.

Lucia opened her eyes, fixed her stare on the crystal ball, and said, "You've gone through trials and disappointments." She shook her head. "Life will begin to treat you fairly."

She looked up at Molly. "You think you were born in the wrong time." Then she turned to me. "You see the spirits of the dead."

Both our legs stopped moving at the same time. Maybe Lucia wasn't a fake.

She continued. "You." She looked at Molly. "Noble blood runs through your veins. Had you lived in another time, you'd feel the power and privilege that provides. But now, 'tis a burden as you fight to keep the old ways alive." Lucia nodded. "Before a year has passed, you will feel the power of being a noblewoman, single-handedly taking care of what belongs to you."

I heard Molly sigh but didn't take my eyes off Lucia as she turned to me. "You are young and don't understand your gift. Few have an open mind about the spirit world. You keep yours closed because you prefer facts. The dead scare you. Don't be afraid. You can help their spirits find peace. That's why they come to you."

"I don't want them coming to me," I whispered.

Lucia shook her head. "It's not your choice. They've selected you."

"No," I whispered. That was not cool.

Lucia smiled at me. "You fool yourself by hiding behind facts and logic. This land, Scotland, runs through your veins. You'll not have the power to fight the pull of its dead. They will speak, and you will listen."

"She only has the gift here in Scotland?" asked Molly.

"Yes," said Lucia. "It's her ancestors calling."

Then she closed her eyes again, moving her hands rhythmically over the crystal ball. Neither Molly nor I was laughing now.

Lucia opened her eyes and focused on Molly again. "You're in love," she said.

Molly stared at her. "I'm a widow."

Lucia smiled. "It's not disloyalty to your first husband to marry another."

"Aye," Molly said.

"Close the gap between the two families," said Lucia. "Your love will do it."

"But—"

Lucia stood. "That is all." The fog stopped. "There is no more to be said." She walked around the table, untied the tent flap, and opened it.

We didn't move.

"That is all," Lucia said, more loudly.

Molly nudged me, and we stood and walked out. While we'd been in the tent, it'd gotten dark. Neither of us said a word. We walked slowly all the way back to Molly's booth and sat down. Fiona and Mom were still gone.

"That was weird," I said, finally finding my voice.

"Aye," Molly said.

"What did she mean by you being in love?"

Molly shook her head. " 'Tis a long story."

"I'll trade you my ghostly tale for your love story," I said.

Molly smiled. "You do like to bargain. Aye, I'll tell ye, Sami. But ye canna say a word to Fiona."

Molly Loves

Laird McClintogg

No wonder she doesn't want Fiona to know.

Talking Ghosts and Love

I don't know how I'm going to get my groove on tonight at the dance. My mind is in overdrive with the whole ghostly-ancestors-talking-to-me stuff and Molly's love for Laird McClintogg.

What do my ghostly ancestors have to say to me? I'm not even really Scottish.

Mom and Fiona Win

Molly had just finished telling me the story of her and Laird McClintogg when Mom and Fiona got back to the booth.

They put us to shame. The two romantics were loaded down with purchases. They had samples of everything from jewelry to small pieces of chain mail.

"What'd you get?" Mom asked.

Molly said, "Oh, we had a lot to chew on."

"I bought small chain-mail bracelets for each of

169

us," said Fiona, handing me one, then putting an identical one on her right wrist. "For the dance tonight."

Interesting jewelry choice.

Highland Dancing

"It's the sword dance," Adan whispered in my ear. He'd changed out of his knight gear and into what he called his evening wear, a more formal outfit consisting mainly of black leather pants.

I watched the girl, no more than twelve, place two swords on the raised platform. She wore a white shirt, a black vest, a plaid skirt, and knee-high socks.

"She'll cross them," Adan said, "and dance."

"Why the swords?" I asked.

Adan's hand sat on my waist, holding me to his side. "It's a dance of dexterity and speed. Historically it was soldiers who danced it. It was a way to train the men in the skill and stamina they'd need for battle."

My jaw dropped as the music began and the dancer leaped into action. It was the most athletic dance I'd ever seen. She jumped and kicked the whole time, staying on the balls of her feet.

When she finished, I was exhausted. "Wow" was all I could manage.

"Aye," Adan said. "It's a powerful dance once done before important battles or as a victory dance. The victor's sword would lie on top of the opponent's. Some legends say that the decapitated head of the loser would be lying next to the swords."

"Okay, gross," I said.

Then he leaned over and kissed me on the lips, right in the middle of the packed market.

Aye.

Day 30

Power Tools

Yesterday Fiona and I finished cleaning the third cottage. Today our moms were with us. Mom and Fiona painted the loft, and I worked with Molly.

She let me use the table saw. That rocked.

"You should just tell Fiona you're dating the laird," I said.

"Aye," she said. "That's what Robert says. I dinnae know how she'll take it, though."

"Does Adan know?" I asked.

"Aye."

"How often do you see the laird?"

"Robert," she said, smiling. "I dinnae call him the laird." She placed a piece of trim along the base of the wall. "We see each other once or twice a week. His wife died three years before Fiona's father."

"There's only one way to find out how Fiona will take it," I said.

Molly nodded. "Aye."

Meeting the Laird

Adan's taking me to his home today. I get to meet his dad, Laird Robert McClintogg. I can't stop cracking my pinky.

Molly told me to relax. Mom laughed. And Fiona just glared at me all morning and mumbled a lot about the devil laird.

By the time Adan picked me up, at six o'clock, I was so nervous I was having bladder issues.

I must've looked pretty bad, because in his car he leaned over and gave me a kiss on the cheek. "Fiona probably told you some things, but he's not a bad man, Sami," he said. "He'll like you."

I didn't tell Adan that I'd yet to have a boyfriend whose parents really liked me. It wasn't that I was hard to get along with or anything; it was just that I felt awkward around some adults, especially when I wanted them to like me.

By the time we pulled up in front of his home, my palms were sweating and my pinky knuckles were begging for mercy. It didn't help that his manor was larger than the White House, complete with turrets and guard towers.

Adan got out, walked around the car, and opened my door. I climbed out. "He'll throw me in the dungeon," I mumbled.

Adan laughed. "Auch, nay . . . maybe put ye on the rack, but not in the dungeon."

I growled, to gain my courage. This was no joking matter, and I was in no mood for his Scottish humor.

"Take a breath, Sami." He leaned over and whispered in my ear. " 'Tis not another girl I've ever brought home. My father will see you're special. Just be yourself, lass."

Okay. I'd be my usual hyperventilating self. Did he say he'd never brought a girl home?

There must be some air around here. Too bad I couldn't get any of it. My head dropped. Geez, I really was going down.

Adan grabbed my waist and moved to my right. "Bend over and breathe," he said.

One . . . two . . . three. Focusing on the numbers calmed me. In a couple more seconds I'd have my confidence back. Four . . . five . . . six.

"What on earth are ye doin' to that bonnie lass, son?"

The voice boomed, and I blacked out.

The Most Embarrassing Moment of My Entire Life

I awoke lying on a leather couch in a huge dark-paneled room. Shelves lined with books were everywhere. Mom sat on a stool beside me.

"There you are, pumpkin," she said.

I saw Adan walk across the room. On one side of him was Molly and on the other side was his father, Laird Robert McClintogg. *So*, I thought, *that's the guy Molly loves?* He was shorter than Adan, but stockier, with lighter hair and a paler complexion.

Then my brain started to catch up with my body. I held my breath. "Don't you dare, Sami Ames," said Mom. "You breathe."

So I did.

"You nearly scared everyone to death," Mom said. "You haven't done that, the whole not breathing thing, since you were six. Remember, it was the first time you were called into the principal's office."

I nodded. Great—not only had I passed out in front of Adan's castle, but Mom was sharing my first trip to the principal's office with everyone.

"Well, lass," said Adan's dad, smiling. "Wish more pretty girls would faint when they see me." He laughed. Dad would call it an honest, good-person laugh.

My throat was dry. I swallowed. "I'm so embarrassed," I said.

"Dinnae be," he said. "Gave me a reason to see Molly MacKensie." He looked at Molly and winked.

Molly blushed and smiled.

I looked at Adan and Mom. Mom winked. "I know," she said.

I sat up, keeping my back propped against the arm of the couch.

"Aye," Molly said. "I was so thrilled with someone knowing that the next day I told your mum."

"We talked about it all day," Mom said. "Like two teenage girls." She laughed.

"Father told me months ago," Adan said.

"So the only one who doesn't know is Fiona?" I asked.

Robert looked at Molly. "Aye." I'm not too quick with some things, but even I could see the flash of hurt in his eyes.

Robert turned to me. "But ye've given Adan and Fiona the opportunity to become friends this summer." He sighed. "That's a step in the right direction."

"I'll tell her, Robert," Molly said.

"Aye," Robert laughed. "Takes a wee lass passing out in my drive to get ye to do it."

"Where is Fiona?" I asked.

"Touring with Margaret, the cook," Adan said.

Trouble...

with a Capital "T"

"Ye stay and rest, lass," Robert said, "as long as ye need to."

I smiled. "Thank you."

He winked. " 'Tis I who should be thanking you. I enjoy reminding my bonnie Molly that she will marry me by the summer's eve."

I watched him smile at Molly. Geez, he really had it bad for her.

"No . . . she . . . will . . . not."

I turned with everyone else to see Fiona standing in the doorway. Her face was white and tears were slowly sliding down her cheeks.

"My mum would rather die than marry a Mc-Clintogg!" she shouted.

I wasn't the only one who stopped breathing then.

"Fiona," Adan said.

"Dinnae speak to me! You're a McClintogg!"

Adan shook his head. "We're friends."

I thought Fiona would break her pinky if she

didn't stop cracking it. "Nay, ye just used me!" she shouted. Her accent was getting stronger.

"How, Fiona?" he asked.

She stammered, "I—I dinnae know . . . but my mum wouldna agree to marry a McClintogg." She turned to Robert. "You're trying to take our farm."

Robert shook his head and opened his arms. "No, lass," he said. "Your father and I were friends."

"Fiona," Molly said. "You've blamed the Mc-Clintoggs for too long. Your father died in an accident. There is no clan feud. You're using a long-dead war to hang on to your father. Robert doesn't want our land."

But Fiona hadn't heard them. She was gone.

Day 33

Fiona Has Run Away

Well, I'm not sure it's technically running away. She took a blanket, a pillow, and a couple days' worth of clothes and moved into the cottage we had spent a week cleaning. It's like she ran away to her basement or something.

Mom and I stayed at the manor house with Molly, trying to keep her calm. She was sure Fiona would hate her forever. I tried thinking like Fiona and came to the conclusion that Fiona wouldn't hate her mom f-o-r-e-v-e-r. Maybe a long time, but not forever. They were too close, and I was sad to see Molly crying. But she didn't go after Fiona.

I told Mom she would've chased me down and dragged me back by my hair. But Mom reminded me that we didn't have other living quarters for me to run to in times of crisis.

I wasn't fooled. Mom is a control freak. She'd go nuts if I left.

But this wasn't about Mom and me.

I'd watched Molly cry for two days. She hadn't smiled, hadn't picked up a power tool; she hadn't even looked at her to-do binder. Robert and Adan stopped by twice. I was really starting to worry.

Fiona was being a whiny baby. She needed to grow up and deal with the fact that her mom wasn't going to stay a widow forever.

Samuel Logan Gave Me an Order

I was sleeping in Fiona's bed when the covers were ripped off me. I woke to see ghost Samuel standing at the foot of the bed with the blankets piled around his feet.

"What do you want?" I asked, rubbing the sleep from my eyes.

"You have to mend this muddle," he whispered.

"What?"

"The families."

"Why are you whispering?"

He shrugged. "It feels right somehow."

I nodded.

"I loved a McClintogg once," he said, "and my bonnie lass loved me. But our families would not let us wed."

"That's stupid," I said.

Samuel looked confused. "I don't understand 'stupid.' "

"Not good," I said.

"Aye," he whispered. "I left to die on a battlefield. I didn't care where or for what cause."

"That sucks."

He looked confused again. "My Annie died within a year of my leaving. 'Tis said she died of a broken heart."

"And you?" I asked.

" 'Tis my shame that when I returned home, I couldn't bear the grief of knowing she was dead, so I took my own life."

I didn't have words. "I'm sorry," I said.

"Put my spirit to rest, Sami, and guide the families to unite. Let love win."

Day 34

Seeing Fiona

I knocked on the door of Fiona's cottage. I'd had it. If Molly wanted to give Fiona time, that was her business, but I knew what I had to do.

"Go away!" Fiona shouted through the door.

I pushed it open. "No!" I yelled, and walked in.

Fiona sat in a chair by the fireplace. It was warm outside, and the roaring fire filled the small room with an almost unbearable heat.

"What are you doing?" I asked.

"Knitting." She held up the needles and yarn and looked at me like I was an idiot for even asking.

She was wearing ragged eighties-style sweats and knitting. This was serious. Not only was she being selfish, she was backsliding into uncool territory.

I glared at her. "Stop being such a jerk," I said, sitting in a chair across from her. "Your mom is totally upset."

She shrugged.

"Fiona." I wanted to shout but kept my voice calm. "This is so stupid."

"Knitting?"

I ignored that. "Fiona." I raised my voice. "Your mom has been crying for two days."

"So have I," she said.

"She says she's giving you space, but if you were my daughter, I'd kick your butt and tell you to grow up."

I thought she was going to jump out of her chair and punch me. "What do you know about it? Your father didn't die. And your mum isn't going to marry a McClintogg."

My patience snapped. "Have you noticed you're the only one who has a problem with the McClintoggs?"

"MacKensies hate them." She caught her breath like she wanted to cry.

"You mean *you* hate them," I said. "And you don't even know why. Robert doesn't want to take your land. He's promised your mom it'll pass down to you."

She smirked. "Aye, and he'll sign it over before they marry?"

I nodded. "He said he would."

She looked confused.

"Truly, Fiona. He seems like a good guy. You're the one being a jerk."

"Am not."

"Oh yeah, you are." I started counting on my fingers. "First you give me all this grief about seeing Adan, but when Shane, Adan, you, and I are all together, you have fun. And you know it.

"Second, do you think your mom would work so hard getting this place into shape if she didn't care about you? She could just marry Robert and move into his castle, you know. But she's making this place work and grow . . . for you." I pointed at her.

"Why didn't she tell me?" Fiona said. "That wasn't right."

I shrugged. "I don't know, Fiona. She probably wishes she had, but in some weird mom way she probably thought she was protecting you or something."

Fiona didn't say anything.

"Third," I continued, "your father was Robert's friend. It wasn't until after your dad—I don't mean to say mean things about the dead, but . . . your dad gambled away the money that should've been used to pay back Robert." I pointed at her again. "And you know that's the truth."

She looked away from me and into the fire. "Aye, but that doesn't make it easier."

"Look, Fiona, you'll always love your dad. He's

gone, though. You're not losing him by letting Robert into your mom's life and maybe someday into yours."

I wished my dad was here. He always knows what to say. I'd like to hug him right now.

"Aye," she said, "but I feel like a traitor to the MacKensies."

"You should be loyal to your mom," I said. "She's the one who's always been loyal to you."

Fiona started crying. "I dinnae know what to do."

"Why?"

"I've been trying for two days to remember why McClintoggs are so bad," she sobbed, "but I can't. Not really. A long time ago they used to steal cattle and sheep from us."

"Do you mean when your dad was a boy?"

"No."

"In the past fifty years?" I asked.

She shook her head. "They used to beat our serfs."

"Good gravy! What, two hundred years ago?"

She nodded. "I know it sounds stupid. But it's our family history that's keeping me from being happy for Mum. And I do want to be, Sami."

"Samuel Logan told me I had to mend things," I said.

"You talked to him again?"

"Yeah." I paced in front of the fire. "He said that he once loved a McClintogg but couldn't marry her because of their families' hatred. A marriage of love between the two families will release his soul."

Fiona shook her head. "That's daft."

I'm not very patient, which is why my friends don't come to me for advice.

"Get over yourself, Fiona," I said. "Your mom won't marry Robert without your blessing."

"She never said one word to me about it," Fiona said.

"Look at you," I said, moving toward the door. "This has made you nuts. Your mom knew it would." I walked to the door. "You're hanging on to stuff based on some long-forgotten feud. This is now. Your mom loves you. Can't you see that?"

I slammed the door on my way out.

Geez, she was so selfish. No wonder Mom sometimes gets mad at me when she thinks I've been selfish. It's annoying.

Day 35

Mother-Daughter Bonding

Fiona was at the main house by 7 a.m. She'd asked Molly to go with her and count sheep.

They've been gone for three hours.

She Said Yes!
She Said Yes!
She Said Yes!

Fiona told her mom it was okay with her if she married Robert.

Wedding Planner

I hope Mom never tries to go into the wedding-planning business. She's unorganized, grouchy, bossy . . . and all about pastels. Isn't Scotland the land of plaids?

I keep trying to tell her that pastels are so last century, even in America. Besides, we're in the Highlands.

"Would you dress one of your characters in pastel for a Highland wedding?" I asked.

She looked at me for so long, I finally knew I had her; I could see it in her eyes.

"Fine," she said. "No pastels." She took a deep breath. "But—"

"No." I waved my hand. "No buts. We're in Scotland. I know Molly is letting you take charge of the wedding details, but you suck at it."

She glared at me. Then the oddest thing happened: she laughed, a snorting, milk-coming-out-of-her-nose laugh.

I watched Mom losing it.

I guess I'm the new wedding planner.

Day 36

Nope

After working on the computer all day making invitations and address labels, printing through one entire cartridge of ink, and licking envelopes, I realized I definitely don't have the patience to be a wedding planner, thank you very much.

It's time-consuming . . . and tastes terrible.

Once Mom had acknowledged the truth about pastels, we called the florist and ordered tons of the darkest red roses on the market. Then Mom, Fiona, and I went to town to shop for dresses.

"Mom will wear her family plaid," said Fiona. "She comes from the Collin clan. The colors are navy blue and tan on a white background."

"I saw the dress yesterday," said Mom. "It reminds me of a Southern belle, the way it's corseted around the top and puffs at the bottom."

"Southern belle?" I asked.

"Dinnae worry, Sami," Fiona said. "It's not lacy and doesn't require three underskirts."

Mom looked at me. "I'm so glad we didn't go pastel."

"Aye," Fiona said. "Pastels are so last century."

I smiled. Fiona was back.

"I will wear the MacKensie colors," Fiona said. "A sash will fall over my right shoulder and go around my waist. A brooch with the MacKensie coat of arms will hold it in place."

"What sort of dress would you like?" Mom asked Fiona.

"Something simple," said Fiona. "MacKensie colors are deep-green plaid over white. Black, I think."

I agreed. Black would look sharp.

"Black," Mom said, stopping midstride. "This is a wedding, Fiona."

"Aye."

"Black?" Mom was horrified.

"It will look chic with the plaid over her shoulder and around her waist," I said. "It's not like she's going to wear a black veil. It'll be classy."

"But—"

"Trust us," Fiona said. "I want Mum's wedding to be special. I'll not go into mourning."

"Black," Mom mumbled, and started walking again. "What should we wear, Sami?"

"I think dark blue or tan to match Molly's plaid," I said.

She nodded. "Well, then. Let's find our dresses."

Day 37

My Dress is So Hot

If Adan doesn't drool all over me when I'm wearing my dress—well, it's technically called a gown—then he's one big loser.

It's light tan, strapless, and has an empire waist. A shimmery, wispy cream fabric lies on top of the tan so I look like I'm floating.

When I tried it on in the dressing room, all three of us agreed it was the dress for me. Mom says it makes me look long and graceful. Fiona says I look like a Greek goddess. How cool is that?

Molly is Nuts

She's getting married in two days, and she's going insane.

It's like watching a grown adult turn into a lovesick teenage weirdo.

Fiona is not far behind. All she keeps talking about is her date, Shane.

I have a date, but I'm not turning into a talks-a-mile-a-minute lunatic.

Mom has a date, too. Dad is coming. He'll be here later tonight. That's so cool. I've been so involved with life here that I've barely mentioned Dad. I've missed him.

Mom and I have made a list of what we want him to see while he's here. Then he'll fly home with us.

We're leaving two days after the wedding. I'm not sure how I feel about that. I've missed my friends, the mall, electricity, running water, Dad, and my bed. But . . . I really like it here.

Day 38

Dad's Here

Dad rented a car and arrived at our cottage early this afternoon. Mom saw the car pull up and ran out the door before he could park. She bounced up and down like a little kid, and when Dad got out she ran and jumped into his arms. He picked her up and spun her around.

I didn't realize how much Mom had missed Dad until they stopped spinning and I saw the tears in her eyes. Dad kissed her on the cheek, put her down, and turned toward me. "Get over here, Sami!" he shouted.

I didn't realize how much *I'd* missed him until I was running toward him with my arms outstretched. He came loping toward me. We must have looked like some dorky commercial or something, running across a field toward each other. He swooped me up into a giant bear hug.

"Ah, I missed my girl," he said.

"I missed you too, Dad."

Dinner

Mom and I had worked all morning on our meal for Dad. We wanted to impress him with our wood-burning-stove cooking skills. We'd made kettle bread, which is called that because it has to cook in a sealed kettle sitting in the coals. We also made potato scones and baked salmon.

Mom wanted to cook a traditional Scottish meal for Dad, so Molly came over yesterday and showed us how to make everything using the coals.

The three of us sat at the table. Mom and Dad couldn't stop smiling. It was weird to see my parents so geeked out over each other.

"You've liked it here, Sami?" Dad asked.

I nodded. "Very much."

He raised his eyebrows and looked at Mom. "Scotland seems to suit her."

Mom laughed. "Probably has something to do with Adan."

I held my breath.

"Adan?" Dad asked.

"Yes," Mom said. "He's the son of Laird Robert McClintogg. Sami has been dating him."

Dad looked at Mom. "And you like this boy?"

"Oh, aye," Mom said.

Dad laughed.

We ate. Mom and I both talked a mile a minute, using a tag-team conversational technique.

I don't know how Dad kept up with our stories, but he did, laughing when he was supposed to and asking questions in the right places.

It was good to be together again.

Day 39

Wedding of the Century

Molly and Robert were married in the chapel in McClintogg Castle. Imagine having a church in your own house. So cool.

Bagpipes sound beautiful when played in a church.

I cried when Fiona placed her mother's hand in Robert's. It was a simple ceremony with only immediate family and Fiona's date, Shane.

Samuel Logan MacKensie was there as well. When I saw his shadow sitting in the last pew, he waved and slowly vanished.

Whew.

Molly looked regal and Robert smiled the entire day.

Adan wore a kilt. He has gorgeous knees.

Dad wore a suit with a plaid tie. Mom tried to get him to wear a kilt, but he refused, saying his bony knees would get cold.

When Adan met Dad, he looked Dad in the eye and shook his hand. I saw the flicker of respect in Dad's eyes.

Adan held my hand all day. Well, except when he was standing at the front of the chapel next to his dad.

I danced with him until the early hours of the morning, making promises to e-mail, text, instant-message, and call.

Fiona said she'd e-mail me copies of all the pictures.

Day 40

Plan to Lure Unsuspecting Tourists and Get Them to Work Our Farm Is Still Moving Forward

Robert hired movers to officially move Molly and Fiona into McClintogg Castle the day after the wedding. Fiona's new room is so awesome. It has a girly four-poster bed with heavy curtains, a fireplace, a window seat, and its own bathroom. I wish I lived in a castle.

MacKensie Castle will be renovated using the income from the tourists who visit the working farm.

Fiona wants to continue to work on the farm while she and Molly fulfill their dream of showing the world medieval Scotland through the operation of MacKensie Manor. Adan and Shane have been enlisted to work at the farm on the weekends, showing tourists how to use medieval weapons.

On Fiona's twentieth birthday, she will officially become head of the MacKensie clan, and MacKensie Manor. She will be Lady MacKensie. I plan to be here for the ceremony.

Good-bye, Samuel

Fiona and I sat on the edge of my bed. The loft was dark. The candle on my nightstand gave off a dim light.

"Do ye think he'll come and say good-bye to you?" asked Fiona.

I shrugged. "I don't know."

We didn't have any of our ghost-hunting gear with us. It was our last night together. I'd be leaving in the morning with my parents.

"I'll miss ye, Sami," Fiona said.

"We'll e-mail," I said.

"Aye." Then I felt Fiona freeze beside me. "Did ye hear that?"

"What?" I whispered.

"Samuel, come out and say farewell to Sami," Fiona said.

A groan rose from the corner. A light mist swirled. I cracked both my pinky knuckles. There was a flash of light, and standing in front of us was Samuel Logan.

I smiled. Fiona whispered to me, "Say something, Sami."

"Hello, Samuel," I said.

He nodded.

Fiona grabbed my arm. "Speak more."

"Are you at peace, Samuel Logan?"

"Aye," he said.

"What did he say, Sami?" asked Fiona. "I can't hear him."

"You can't?"

"No."

I nodded. "He's at peace."

"Aye," Fiona whispered. "Good. Is he with his lovely McClintogg lass?"

Samuel smiled. "Aye, tell her I am. But I've come to say my final good-bye, lass," he said. "I've waited a century for someone to bring the clans back together, and ye have. Now the families will grow and prosper once again."

I shook my head. "I didn't do anything."

"Aye, ye did. Ye helped join the MacKensies and

McClintoggs. I was too weak. They're joined now, and I can rest in peace."

"What's he saying?" Fiona asked.

"Shhh."

Samuel looked at Fiona. "That lass will lead us into the future along with her new kin, Adan. The clans are at peace and will prosper."

There was another flash of light, and he was gone.

"What did he say, Sami?" Fiona asked.

I turned and looked at her. "He said that you and Adan will bring the MacKensie and McClintogg clans back, and he can rest now."

"His spirit has moved on, then?"

"Definitely."

Day 41

Going Home

Mom has filled a notebook with enough fodder to write a trilogy.

I cried.

Mom cried.

Molly cried.

Fiona cried.

We had a soggy group hug.

Dad shook Laird McClintogg's hand.

Adan hugged and kissed me in front of Mom and Dad. They smiled.

The new McClintogg clan has invited us for the Christmas holidays. Mom and Dad said we'd come.

I'll miss my school's winter formal, but who cares? Mine will be the Christmas Ball at McClintogg Castle.

I don't have to make up a story about some boyfriend in a foreign country because I really have one. And he's one hot Scot.

100 Days to Work on My Entrance into the McClintogg Christmas Ball